GREAT ILLUSTRATED

Fairy Tales

LITTLE RED RIDING HOOD
GOLDILOCKS AND THE THREE BEARS
THE THREE LITTLE PIGS
AND OTHER STORIES

Adapted by Rochelle Larkin

Illustrated by Jesse Zerner

BARONET BOOKS
NEW YORK, NEW YORK

TABLE *of* CONTENTS

"A Basket of All Good Things"

LITTLE · RED · RIDING · HOOD

Once upon a time a little girl lived with her mother in a neat cottage at the edge of a forest. She was a good little girl, and everybody liked her; but no one so much as her grandmother. Grandmother, who lived all the way on the other side of the forest, had made the little girl a beautiful red cape for her birthday. The little girl so loved this gift that she wore it all the time, so much so that people all called her Little Red Riding Hood, so much so that her old real name was quite forgotten!

One day, as Little Red Riding Hood was playing in the grassy space in front of the cottage, her mother called her inside.

"Grandma is not feeling well and cannot leave her house," Little Red Riding Hood's mother said. "I'm packing a basket of all good things for you to take to her."

Little Red Riding Hood skipped with joy. She loved walking in the woods, and she loved going to her grandmother's house.

"Now, Little Red Riding Hood," her mother went on, "you must go straight to Grandma's and not stop for anything. Do not play in the woods and above all, you must not speak to any strangers."

Little Red Riding Hood promised, and tucking the basket under her arm, off she went.

The forest was especially beautiful that morning. The sun shone through the glades of trees, splashing its touches of gold everywhere. Little animals of the forest, rabbits and squirrels and chipmunks, scampered everywhere. Little flowers poked out from the ground and spread their petals in appreciation of the sun's warm rays.

Little Red Riding Hood marched along merrily. She kept straight on the path to her grandma's, humming a little song to herself as she went. Suddenly a flash of bright color caught her eye. She stopped, and stooped to look. It was a beautiful purple flower, one she had never seen in the forest before. She leaned over, admiring it, and trying to count the others like it that were just pushing their heads through the warming soil.

"Good morning, Little Red Riding Hood!" boomed a voice suddenly.

Little Red Riding Hood jumped up, startled. She grew even more frightened when she saw that the voice belonged to an enormous wolf, who stood towering over her.

"It's a beautiful morning, isn't it?" boomed the wolf. "Don't you think so, Little Red Riding Hood?"

Little Red Riding Hood was amazed that the wolf knew her

"Good Morning, Little Red Riding Hood!"

name. "And aren't these beautiful flowers?" the wolf said. "I see you've been admiring them, too."

Little Red Riding Hood nodded. If the wolf, who had such a bad reputation, liked flowers, maybe he wasn't so bad as she had heard after all.

"I'm sure you'd like to pick some to take with you," the wolf said. "I'm sure your mother would like to see them, too."

"But I'm not going home now," said Little Red Riding Hood, forgetting completely what her mother had told her. "I'm going to see my grandma. She's sick and can't leave her house."

"All the more reason to pick some," the wolf said, his voice not sounding so loud and frightening anymore.

"That's a good idea," said Little Red Riding Hood, "I'll just stop long enough to get some flowers for grandma."

"What a good little girl you are!" said the wolf approvingly. "It's always such a pleasure to meet such a polite young lady!" He took off his large feathered hat and swept down in a low bow before Little Red Riding Hood. "I hope we may meet again soon," he said as he turned to go.

"Yes, to be sure," said Little Red Riding Hood, more out of politeness than the wish to ever see him again. Although, she thought, as she knelt down on the warm earth to gather the purple blossoms, perhaps the wolf was not such a terrible creature after all.

But no sooner had the wolf left Little Red Riding Hood, that

"Some Flowers for Grandma"

he hastened as fast as he could to her grandmother's house.

There he stood on the doorstep, knocking lightly.

"Who is there?" called the grandmother from inside. "Is it you, Little Red Riding Hood?"

"Yes," replied the wolf in a soft, wavery-quavery voice, trying to sound as much like a little girl as he could manage.

"Come in, come in, my dear," called Little Red Riding Hood's grandmother from inside.

Quickly the wolf threw open the door and went into the house. When she saw the wolf, Grandmother shrieked and fell back on the bed. But the wolf pulled her off very roughly and threw her into the closet. Then, rummaging among her things, he picked out a long nightdress and matching cap and quickly got himself into them. Then he snuggled under the bedclothes, hiding as much of himself as possible, and waited for Little Red Riding Hood to appear.

It didn't take long. "Grandma, are you there?" called Little Red Riding Hood from just outside the door.

"Yes I am," called out the wolf, trying to sound as grandma-like as he could. "Come right in, my dear!"

Little Red Riding Hood skipped happily into the room. "Look at all of these good things that Mama has sent for you," she said, putting the basket on the table. "And look at these beautiful purple flowers I brought for you!"

She turned to give the flowers to her grandmother, but was

Snuggled Under the Bedclothes

startled at how strange she looked.

"Why grandmother, what big eyes you have!" said Little Red Riding Hood.

"The better to see you with, my dear," said the wolf, in the very best grandma-voice he could manage.

"But—but grandma," Little Red Riding Hood stammered, "what big ears you have!"

"The better to hear you with, my dear," cackled the wolf, trying to make a grandma's laugh. "Now come closer, my darling, so I can see and hear you all the better.

Little Red Riding Hood walked toward the bed very slowly.

"But grandma," said Little Red Riding Hood, "what big teeth you have!"

"The better to eat you with, my dear!" shouted the wolf, tearing out of the grandmother's clothes and leaping toward Little Red Riding Hood.

She started screaming as loud as she could.

Luckily, there was a woodsman working in the forest nearby, and he heard her cries and calls for help. Hatchet in hand, he strode quickly toward the little house, threw open the door, and stepped inside just as the wolf was about to grasp Little Red Riding Hood in his long, hideous claws.

Thwack! Thwack! Two blows from the woodsman's hatchet and the wolf let go of Little Red Riding Hood and fell to the floor.

"The Better to Eat You with, My Dear!"

There was a loud banging from inside the closet. The woodsman stepped over the wolf and released Little Red Riding Hood's real grandmother.

They hugged and kissed each other gratefully, and heartily thanked the woodsman for all he had done for them.

Then the three of them sat down at the table to enjoy the basket of goodies that Little Red Riding Hood's mother had prepared.

And although Little Red Riding Hood was to visit her grandmother many, many times again, never did she ever stop in the forest or anywhere else to speak to strangers.

Enjoying the Goodies

Goldilocks Saw the Porridge.

Goldilocks · And · The · Three · Bears

Once upon a time, deep in a forest, lived a family of bears — a Papa Bear, a Mama Bear, and a little Baby Bear.

Every morning, Mama Bear made porridge. All the bears loved porridge. But one morning when the porridge was too hot, the bears decided to take a walk in the forest while it cooled off.

While they were gone, a little girl named Goldilocks came by. She had never seen the bears' cottage before, and she was very curious. Seeing that nobody was inside, she went in to look around.

Goldilocks saw the porridge on the table. She tasted the Papa Bear's porridge, but it was too hot. Then she tasted the Mama Bear's, but it was too cold. She tasted the Baby Bear's porridge and it was just right, so she ate it all up.

Goldilocks went into the parlor. She sat down in the Papa Bear's rocking chair, but it was too hard. She sat down in the Mama Bear's rocking chair, but it was too soft. Then she sat down in the Baby Bear's rocking chair, and it was just right!

But Baby Bear's rocking chair was too small for Goldilocks,

and she broke it all to pieces.

Goldilocks decided to go upstairs. It would be nice to take a little nap, she thought. First she tried Papa Bear's bed; it was too hard.

Then she tried the Mama Bear's bed. It was too soft.

Goldilocks tried Baby Bear's bed and it was just right! She snuggled under the covers and fell fast asleep.

In a little while, the bears came home.

"Somebody's been eating my porridge!" said the Papa Bear.

"Somebody's been eating my porridge!" said the Mama Bear.

"Somebody's been eating my porridge, and ate it all up!" cried the Baby Bear.

The bears went into the parlor.

"Somebody's been sitting in my chair!" said the Papa Bear.

"Somebody's been sitting in my chair!" said the Mama Bear.

"Somebody's been sitting in my chair, and broke it all to pieces!" said the Baby Bear and he began to cry again.

The three bears went upstairs.

"Somebody's been sleeping in my bed!" said the Papa Bear.

"Somebody's been sleeping in my bed!" said the Mama Bear.

"Somebody's been sleeping in my bed," said the Baby Bear, "and there she is!"

Goldilocks jumped up. She was so frightened she ran down the stairs and ran out of the house before the bears could even move.

And they never saw or heard from Goldilocks ever again.

"And There She Is!"

"My Gingerbread Boy!"

THE · GINGERBREAD · MAN

Once upon a time a little old man and a little old woman lived all alone in a little old house. They didn't have any children and were often lonely.

One day the little old woman had an idea. As she was quite clever about the kitchen, she shaped a little boy out of gingerbread. She used two raisins for his eyes, and a little red cherry for his mouth. She sprinkled shredded coconut on his head for hair, and dressed him in a suit all of chocolate, with little round hazelnuts for buttons. For feet, she attached two large brown nuts. When all was ready, she patted him into shape and put him in the oven to be done.

When at last he was finished, the little old woman was overjoyed with the results. "He is my own, my gingerbread boy!" she said.

But as she took him out of the oven, the gingerbread boy jumped out of the pan and onto the floor, through the little house and out into the street.

The old woman and the old man tried to catch him, running as fast as they could down the street.

The old woman begged and begged for him to stop, but the gingerbread boy only laughed.

"Run, run, run, fast as you can
You'll never catch the gingerbread man!"
And they couldn't.

The gingerbread boy ran all the way out of town, until he was quite in the countryside. A cow, eating grass beside the road, saw him. That would be nice to eat, she thought, a change from only grass. "Stop," said the cow to the gingerbread boy. "I would like to eat you." But the little gingerbread boy only laughed as he ran.

"Run, run, run, fast as you can
You'll never catch the gingerbread man!"
he called as he ran past.

The cow sighed. Even running on all of her four legs, she knew she couldn't run as fast as the gingerbread boy did on his two. So the cow stayed in her place and the gingerbread boy ran on, ever faster.

He ran until he came upon a horse in a pasture. The horse was getting tired of the same bucket of oats day after day, and this little gingerbread boy, he thought, looked good enough to eat.

"Stop, little gingerbread boy," called out the horse.

But the gingerbread boy kept on running.

"Run, run, run, fast as you can

"Stop," Said the Cow.

You'll never catch the gingerbread man!"
called out the gingerbread boy.

The horse could run fast, much faster than the cow, but the gingerbread boy was running like the wind, and the horse stayed behind with his oats.

Soon he came to the barn. When the threshers who were piling the hay inside sniffed the air and the good, spicy smell of the gingerbread boy, they stopped working, and called out to him to stop. "Why are you running so fast, little gingerbread boy?" they asked. "Why don't you stop and rest with us for a while?"

But the little gingerbread boy just smiled with his little cherry mouth and kept on running.

"Run, run, run, fast as you can

You'll never catch the gingerbread man!"
shouted the gingerbread boy.

Beyond the pastures and the barn was a field full of mowers. They too thought that the little gingerbread boy would make a fine dessert.

"Stop him, stop him!" some of the mowers called to others who were closer to the road.

But the little gingerbread just laughed at all their attempts at catching him. Like the wind he went, and he sang out as he ran:

"Run, run, run, fast as you can

You'll never catch the gingerbread man!"
Having outrun all he had met thus far, the proud little ginger-

"Run, Run, Run, Fast As You Can!"

bread boy was sure that he could outrun and outsmart anybody in the world. When he saw a fox crossing through the next field, the gingerbread boy didn't worry a bit.

When the fox began to run quickly toward him, the little gingerbread boy was not afraid. "You can't catch me!" he sang out merrily and ran as fast as he could.

But soon he came to a river that ran at the far end of the farm. The little gingerbread boy did not know how to swim, and the water looked very wet, not at all the sort of thing that was good for a person such as himself.

Still, he had to find a way to get across. The people and the horse and the cow might still catch up to him if he didn't.

Up came the fox. "If you get up on my tail," said the fox, "I'll get you across this river perfectly safely."

Then the little gingerbread boy jumped right on, and into the river swam the fox.

They had gone just a little way when the fox turned round to face him. "The water is getting much deeper," said the fox, "I think it would be better for you to get on my back, so you don't get wet."

The little gingerbread boy crawled onto the fox's back, holding to his fur as fast as he could.

When they were almost to the opposite shore, the fox turned round again. "You are going to get too wet on my back," he said. "It would be far better if you jumped up here on my head."

"Get on My Tail."

And so they went on for a while, the gingerbread boy not noticing how long it was taking to reach the shore.

Then, the fox tipped back his muzzle and spoke to the gingerbread boy who was perched on top of the fox's head. "You are still getting too wet, being up there," said the fox. "I think you had better come forward, my little friend, and crawl out here on my nose."

Just as the little gingerbread boy did so, they reached the bank of the river. The fox threw his head back, and he snapped the little gingerbread boy right into his mouth.

And the fast, proud little gingerbread boy was never seen or heard from again.

The Fox Snapped His Mouth.

Each in a Different Direction

THE · THREE · LITTLE · PIGS

O nce upon a time there were three little pigs who lived with their mother. One day, she decided it was time for her three sons to go out on their own.

She gathered them to her. "Listen, my children," she said, "you are all of an age to make your own ways in the world. Go with my blessing and always remember this: beware of wolves. They are our enemies and they can do you much harm."

The three little pigs packed up their belongings and each went off in a different direction.

The first little pig was walking along his chosen road when he met a man hitching large piles of hay. The little pig had an idea.

"This must be my lucky day,
I can build my house of hay!"

He gave the man some of the coins his mother had tucked carefully into his pouch, and off he went to build his house.

The little pig worked very hard and at last the house was done. He had just settled in to have a nice cup of tea when he heard a terrible noise outside.

It was a wolf!

"Little pig, little pig, let me come in!"

"Not by the hair of my chinny chin chin," cried the little pig.

"Then I'll huff and I'll puff
and I'll blow your house in!"
yelled the wolf.

He huffed and he puffed and in one great breath, the wolf blew down the little house of hay.

The little pig ran out as quickly as he could, and went to look for his brothers.

The second little pig was walking along a road when he met a man who had a great wagon load of wood.

"This is something very good,
I think I'll build my house of wood!"
said the little pig.

He paid the man for the whole wagonload of wood and set off to build his house.

The little pig liked his house of sturdy sticks, and he settled in to enjoy himself.

But it wasn't long before he heard a terrible howling outside his window.

"Little pig, little pig,
let me come in!"
called the wolf.

"I'll Huff and I'll Puff!"

"Not by the hair of my chinny chin chin!"
cried out the little pig.

"Then I'll huff and puff
and I'll blow your house in!"
called the wolf.

He huffed and he puffed and he puffed and he huffed and at last the little house of wood fell all to pieces.

The little pig ran away as fast as he could to look for his brothers.

The third little pig was on his way when he saw a man with a great load of bricks.

"I'll have walls so safe and thick
if I build my house of brick!"
thought the third little pig.

He carted off the whole load of bricks and worked very carefully to build his big, strong house.

And just in time! For here came his two brothers, running quickly from opposite directions. The strong brick house was big enough for all of them, and the three little pigs settled in very happily.

The third little pig had just put up a big kettle of soup for their dinner when from outside came such a howling and rumbling that even the windowpanes of the sturdy brick house shook.

"Little pigs, little pigs,
let me come in!"
shouted the wolf.

"And I'll Blow Your House In!"

"Not by the hairs of our chinny chin chins!"
shouted back the pigs.

"Then I'll huff and I'll puff

and I'll blow your house in!"
shouted the wolf.

He huffed and he puffed and he puffed and he huffed and he puffed and he huffed some more, but the wolf could not blow down the sturdy brick house!

The wolf was getting very angry. He knew that the three little pigs were safe inside. He could not blow down the house of bricks. He had to think of something else.

The wolf looked around carefully. He saw the chimney on top of the house. "Ah ha," he thought, "I can climb up there. Then I'll slide down the chimney and be inside the house."

It was very quiet, and the three little pigs thought that the wolf had gone away. But then they heard a scampering, scratching sound above them. They knew the wolf was on the roof.

The third little pig stirred and stoked the fire under the big kettle. Soon he had a roaring blaze going. That would make a warm welcome indeed for the big bad wolf!

Soon enough, down came the wolf. Right into the boiling kettle he went.

And what do you think the three little pigs had for supper that night? Wolf soup! Plus, with no big bad wolf to bother them anymore, the three little pigs lived happily ever after.

Wolf Soup!

The Kingdom of Joyous Land

THE · JOLLY · KING'S · DAUGHTER

Once upon a time there lived a King and Queen who loved each other so much that they were never happy unless they were together. Day after day they went out hunting or fishing; night after night they went to balls or to the opera; they sang, and danced, and ate sugarplums, and were the happiest of the happy, and all their subjects followed their example so that the kingdom was called the Joyous Land.

Now in the next kingdom everything was as different as it could possibly be. The King was sulky and savage, and never enjoyed himself at all. He looked so ugly and cross that all his subjects feared him, and he hated the very sight of a cheerful face, so if he ever caught anyone smiling he had his head cut off that very minute. This kingdom was very appropriately called the Land of Tears.

Now when this wicked King heard of the happiness of the jolly King, he was so jealous that he collected a great army and set out to fight him, and the news of his approach was soon brought to the jolly King and his Queen.

The Queen, when she heard of it, was frightened out of her wits, and began to cry bitterly. "Sire," she said, "let us collect all our riches and run away as far as ever we can, to the other side of the world!"

But the King answered:

"Fie, madam! I am far too brave for that. It is better to die than to be a coward."

Then he assembled all his armed men, and after bidding the Queen a tender farewell, he mounted his splendid horse and rode away. When he was lost to sight, the Queen could do nothing but weep, and wring her hands, and cry.

"Alas! If the King is killed, what will become of me and of my little daughter?" and she was so sorrowful that she could neither eat nor sleep.

The King sent her a letter every day, but at last, one morning, as she looked out of the palace window, she saw a messenger approaching in hot haste.

"What news, courier? What news?" cried the Queen, and he answered:

"The battle is lost and the King is dead, and in another moment the enemy will be here."

The poor Queen fell back insensible, and all her ladies carried her to bed, and stood round her weeping and wailing. Then began a tremendous noise and confusion, and they knew that the enemy had arrived, and very soon they heard the wicked King himself

He Mounted His Splendid Horse.

stamping about the palace seeking the Queen.

Then her ladies put the little Princess into her arms, and covered her up, head and all, in the bedclothes, and ran for their lives, and the poor Queen lay there shaking and hoping she would not be found. But very soon the wicked King clattered into the room, and in a fury because the Queen would not answer when he called to her, he tore back her silken coverings and her lace cap, and when all her lovely hair came tumbling down over her shoulders, he wound it three times round his hand and threw her over his shoulder, where he carried her like a sack of flour.

The poor Queen held her little daughter safe in her arms and shrieked for mercy, but the wicked King only mocked her, and begged her to go on shrieking, as it amused him, and he mounted his great horse, and rode back to his own country. When he got there he declared that he would have the Queen and the little Princess hanged on the nearest tree; but his courtiers said that seemed a pity, for when the baby grew up she would be a very nice wife for the King's only son.

The King was rather pleased with this idea, and shut the Queen up in the highest room of a tall tower, which was very tiny, and miserably furnished with a table and a very hard bed upon the floor. Then he sent for a fairy who lived near his kingdom, and after receiving her with more politeness than he generally showed, and entertaining her at a sumptuous feast, he took her up to see the Queen.

Like a Sack of Flour!

The fairy was so touched by the sight of her misery that when she kissed her hand she whispered:

"Courage, madam! I think I see a way to help you."

The Queen, a little comforted by these words, received her graciously, and begged her to take pity upon the poor little Princess, who had met with such a sudden reverse of fortune.

But the King got very cross when he saw them whispering together, and cried harshly:

"Make an end of these fine speeches, madam. I brought you here to tell me if the child will grow up pretty and fortunate."

Then the fairy answered that the Princess would be as pretty, and clever, and well brought up as it was possible to be, and the King growled to the Queen that it was lucky for her that it was so, as they would certainly have been hanged if it were otherwise. Then he stamped off, taking the fairy with him, and leaving the poor Queen in tears.

"How can I wish my little daughter to grow up pretty if she is to be married to that horrid little dwarf, the King's son," she said to herself, "and yet, if she is ugly we shall both be killed. If I could only hide her away somewhere so that the wicked King could never find her."

As the days went on, the Queen and the little Princess grew thinner and thinner, for their hard-hearted jailer gave them every day only three boiled peas and a tiny morsel of black bread, so they were always terribly hungry. At last, one evening, as the Queen sat

"Courage, Madam!"

at her spinning-wheel — for the King was so stingy that she was made to work day and night — she saw a tiny, pretty little mouse creep out of a hole, and said to it:

"Alas, little creature! what are you coming to look for here? I only have three peas for my day's provision, so unless you wish to fast you must go elsewhere."

But the mouse ran hither and thither, and danced and capered so prettily, that at last the Queen gave it her last pea, saying, "Here, little one, eat it up; I have nothing better to offer you, but I give this willingly in return for the amusement I have had from you."

She had hardly spoken when she saw upon the table a delicious little roast partridge, and two dishes of preserved fruit. "Truly," said she, "a kind action never goes unrewarded"; and she and the little Princess ate their supper with great satisfaction, and then the Queen gave what was left to the little mouse, who danced better than ever afterwards.

The next morning came the jailer with the Queen's allowance of three peas, which he brought in upon a large dish to make them look even smaller; but as soon as he set it down the little mouse came and ate up all three, so that when the Queen wanted her dinner there was nothing left for her. She was quite provoked, and said:

"What a bad little beast that mouse must be! If it goes on like this I shall be starved." But when she glanced at the dish again it

"Kind Action Never Goes Unrewarded."

was covered with all sorts of nice things to eat, and the Queen had a very good dinner, and was happier than usual over it. But afterwards as she sat at her spinning-wheel she began to consider what would happen if the little Princess did not grow up pretty enough to please the King, and she said to herself:

"Oh if I could only think of some way of escaping."

As she spoke she saw the little mouse playing in a corner with some long straws. The Queen took them and began to braid them, saying:

"If only I had straws enough I would make a basket with them, and let my baby down in it from the window to any kind passerby who would take care of her."

By the time the straws were all braided, the little mouse had dragged in more and more, until the Queen had enough to make her basket, and she worked at it day and night, while the little mouse danced for her amusement; and at meal time the Queen gave it the three peas and the bit of black bread, and always found something good in the dish in their place. She really could not imagine where all the nice things came from.

At last one day when the basket was finished, the Queen was looking out of the window to see how long a cord she must make to lower it to the bottom of the tower, when she noticed a little old woman who was leaning upon her stick and looking up at her. Presently she said:

"I know your trouble, madam. If you like I will help you."

"If I Only Had Straws Enough . . ."

"Oh! my dear friend," said the Queen. "If you really wish to be of use to me, you will come at the time that I will appoint, and I will let down my poor little baby in a basket. If you will take her, and bring her up for me, when I am rich I will reward you splendidly."

"I don't care about the reward," said the old woman, "but there is one thing I should like. You must know that I am very particular about what I eat, and if there is one thing that I fancy above all others, it is a plump, tender little mouse. If there is such a thing in your garret just throw it down to me, and in return I will promise that your little daughter shall be well taken care of."

The Queen when she heard this began to cry, but made no answer, and the old woman, after waiting a few minutes, asked her what was the matter.

"Why," said the Queen, "there is only one mouse in this garret, and that is such a dear, pretty little thing that I cannot bear to think of its being killed."

"What!" cried the old woman, in a rage. "Do you care more for a miserable mouse than for your own baby? Good-bye, madam! I leave you to enjoy its company, and for my own part I thank my stars that I can get plenty of mice without troubling you to give them to me."

And she hobbled off grumbling and growling. As to the Queen, she was so disappointed that, in spite of finding a better dinner than usual, and seeing the little mouse dancing in its

"You Care More for a Mouse..."

merriest mood, she could do nothing but cry. That night when her baby was fast asleep she packed it into the basket, and wrote on a slip of paper, "This unhappy little girl is called Delicia!" This she pinned to its robe, and then very sadly she was shutting the basket, when in sprang the little mouse and sat on the baby's pillow.

"Ah! little one," said the Queen, "it cost me dear to save your life. How shall I know now whether my Delicia is being taken care of or not? Anyone else would have let the greedy old woman have you, and eat you up, but I could not bear to do it."

Whereupon the mouse answered:

"Believe me, madam, you will never repent of your kindness."

The Queen was immensely astonished when the mouse began to speak, and still more so when she saw its little sharp nose turn to a beautiful face, and its paws to hands and feet; then it suddenly grew tall, and the Queen recognized the fairy who had come with the wicked King to visit her.

The fairy smiled at her astonished look, and said:

"I wanted to see if you were faithful and capable of feeling real friendship for me, for you see we fairies are rich in everything but friends, and those are hard to find."

"It is not possible that *you* should want for friends, you charming creature," said the Queen.

"Indeed it is so," the fairy said. "For those who are only friendly with me for their own advantage, I do not count at all. But when you cared for the poor little mouse you could not have

"You Will Never Repent."

known there was anything to be gained by it, and to try you further I took the form of the old woman whom you talked to from the window, and then I was convinced that you really loved me."

Then, turning to the little Princess, she kissed her rosy lips three times, saying:

"Dear little one, I promise that you shall be richer than your father, and shall live a hundred years, always pretty and happy, without fear of old age and wrinkles."

The Queen, quite delighted, thanked the fairy gratefully, and begged her to take charge of the little Delicia and bring her up as her own daughter. This she agreed to do, and then they shut the basket and lowered it carefully, baby and all, to the ground at the foot of the tower. The fairy then changed herself back into the form of a mouse, and this delayed her a few seconds, after which she ran nimbly down the straw rope, but only to find when she got to the bottom that the baby had disappeared.

In the greatest terror she ran up again to the Queen, crying:

"All is lost! My enemy Cancaline has stolen the Princess away. You must know that she is a cruel fairy who hates me, and as she is older than I am and has more power, I can do nothing against her. I know no way of rescuing Delicia from her clutches."

When the Queen heard this terrible news she was heartbroken, and begged the fairy to do all she could to get the poor little Princess back again. At this moment in came the jailer, and when he missed the little Princess he at once told the King, who

Taking Charge of Little Delicia

came in a great fury asking what the Queen had done with her.

She answered that a fairy, whose name she did not know, had come and carried her off by force.

Upon hearing this the King stamped upon the ground, and cried in a terrible voice:

"You shall be hung! I always told you you should." And without another word he dragged the unlucky Queen out into the nearest wood, and climbed up into a tree to look for a branch from which he could hang her.

But when he was quite high up, the fairy, who had made herself invisible and followed them, gave him a sudden push, which made him lose his footing and fall to the ground with a crash and break four of his teeth, and while he was trying to mend them the fairy carried the Queen off in her flying chariot to a beautiful castle, where she was so kind to her that but for the loss of Delicia the Queen would have been perfectly happy.

But though the good little mouse did her very utmost, they could not find out where Cancaline had hidden the little Princess.

Thus fifteen years went by, and the Queen had somewhat recovered from her grief, when the news reached her that the son of the wicked King wished to marry the little maiden who kept the turkeys, and that she had refused him; the wedding dresses had been made, nevertheless, and the festivities were to be so splendid that all the people for miles round were flocking in to be at them.

The Queen felt quite curious about a little turkey-maiden

The Fairy Gave Him a Sudden Push.

who did not wish to be a Queen, so the little mouse conveyed herself to the poultry-yard to find out what she was like.

She found the turkey-maiden sitting upon a big stone, bare-footed, and miserably dressed in an old, coarse linen gown and cap; the ground at her feet was all strewn with robes of gold and silver, ribbons and laces, diamonds and pearls, over which the turkeys were stalking to and fro, while the King's disagreeable son stood opposite her, declaring angrily that if she would not marry him she should be killed.

The turkey-maiden answered proudly:

"I never will marry you! You are much like your cruel father. Leave me in peace with my turkeys, which I like far better than all your fine gifts."

The little mouse watched her with the greatest admiration, for she was as beautiful as the spring; and as soon as the wicked Prince was gone, she took the form of an old peasant woman and said to her:

"Good-day, my pretty one! You have a fine flock of turkeys there."

The young turkey-maiden turned her gentle eyes upon the old woman, and answered:

"Yet they wish me to leave them to become a miserable Queen! What is your advice upon the matter?"

"My child," said the fairy, "a crown is a very pretty thing, but you know neither the price nor the weight of it."

"I Will Never Marry You!"

"I know so well that I have refused to wear one," said the little maiden, "though I don't know who was my father, or who was my mother, and I have not a friend in the world."

"You have goodness and beauty, which are of more value than ten kingdoms," said the wise fairy. "But tell me, child, how came you here, and how is it you have neither father, nor mother, nor friend?"

"A fairy called Cancaline is the cause of my being here," answered the girl, "for while I lived with her I got nothing but blows and harsh words, until at last I could bear it no longer, and ran away from her without knowing where I was going, and as I came through a wood the wicked Prince met me, and offered to give me charge of the poultry-yard. I accepted gladly, not knowing that I should have to see him day by day. And now he wants to marry me, but that I will never consent to."

Upon hearing this the fairy became convinced that the little turkey-maiden was none other than the Princess Delicia.

"What is your name, my little one?" said she.

"I am called Delicia, if it please you," she answered.

Then the fairy threw her arms round the Princess's neck, and nearly smothered her with kisses, saying:

"Ah, Delicia! I am a very old friend of yours, and I am truly glad to find you at last; but you might look nicer than you do in that old gown, which is only fit for a kitchen-maid. Take this pretty dress and let us see the difference it will make."

"Delicia, If It Please You . . ."

So Delicia took off the ugly cap, and shook out all her fair, shining hair, and bathed her hands and face in clear water from the nearest spring till her cheeks were like roses, and when she was adorned with the diamonds and the splendid robe the fairy had given her, she was the most beautiful Princess in the world, and the fairy with great delight cried:

"Now you look as you ought to look, Delicia, what do you think about it yourself?"

And Delicia answered:

"I feel as if I were the daughter of some great king."

"And would you be glad if you were?" said the fairy.

"Indeed I should," answered she.

"Ah, well," said the fairy, "tomorrow I may have some pleasant news for you."

So she hurried back to her castle, where the Queen sat busy with her embroidery, and cried:

"Well madam, will you wager your thimble and your golden needle that I am bringing you the best news you could possibly hear?"

"Alas!" sighed the Queen, "since the death of the jolly King and the loss of my Delicia, all the news in the world is not worth a pin to me."

"There, there, don't be melancholy," said the fairy. "I assure you the Princess is quite well, and I have never seen her equal for beauty. She might be a Queen tomorrow if she chose"; and then

The Most Beautiful Princess in the World

she told all that had happened, and the Queen first rejoiced over the thought of Delicia's beauty, and then wept at the idea of her being a turkey-maiden.

"I will not hear of her being made to marry the wicked King's son," she said. "Let us go at once and bring her here."

In the meantime the wicked Prince, who was very angry with Delicia, had sat himself down under a tree, and cried and howled with rage and spite until the King heard him, and cried out from the window:

"What is the matter with you, that you are making all this disturbance?"

The Prince replied:

"It is all because our turkey-maiden will not love me!"

"Won't love you?" said the King. "We'll very soon see about that!" So he called his guards and told them to go and fetch Delicia. "See if I don't make her change her mind pretty soon!" said the wicked King with a chuckle.

Then the guards began to search the poultry-yard, and could find nobody there but Delicia, who, with her splendid dress and her crown of diamonds, looked such a lovely Princess that they hardly dared to speak to her. But she said to them very politely:

"Pray tell me what you are looking for here?"

"Madam," they answered, "we are sent for an insignificant little person called Delicia."

"The Turkey-Maiden Will Not Love Me!"

"Alas!" said she, "that is my name. What can you want with me?"

So the guards tied her hands and feet with thick ropes, for fear she might run away, and brought her to the King, who was waiting with his son.

When he saw her he was very much astonished at her beauty, which would have made anyone less hard-hearted sorry for her. But the wicked King only laughed and mocked at her, and cried, "Well, little fright, little toad! Why don't you love my son, who is far too handsome and too good for you? Make haste and begin to love him this instant, or you shall be tarred and feathered."

Then the poor little Princess, shaking with terror, went down on her knees, crying:

"Oh, don't tar and feather me, please! It would be so uncomfortable. Let me have two or three days to make up my mind, and then you shall do as you like with me."

The wicked Prince would have liked very much to see her tarred and feathered, but the King ordered that she should be shut up in a dark dungeon. It was just at this moment that the Queen and the fairy arrived in the flying chariot, and the Queen was dreadfully distressed at the turn affairs had taken, and said miserably that she was destined to be unfortunate all her days. But the fairy bade her take courage.

"I'll pay them out yet," said she, nodding her head with an air of great determination.

"Why Don't You Love My Son?"

That very same night, as soon as the wicked King had gone to bed, the fairy changed herself into the little mouse, and creeping up on to his pillow nibbled his ear, so that he squealed out quite loudly and turned over on his other side; but that was no good, for the little mouse only set to work and gnawed away at the other ear until it hurt more than the first one.

Then the King cried, "Murder!" and "Thieves!" and all his guards ran to see what was the matter, but they could find nothing and nobody, for the little mouse had run off to the Prince's room and was serving him in exactly the same way. All night long she ran from one to the other, until at last, driven quite frantic by terror and want of sleep, the King rushed out of the palace crying, "Help! Help! I am pursued by rats."

The Prince when he heard this got up also, and ran after the King, and they had not gone far when they both fell into the river and were never heard of again.

Then the good fairy ran to tell the Queen, and they went together to the dungeon where Delicia was imprisoned. The fairy touched each door with her wand, and it sprang open instantly, but they had to go through forty before they came to the Princess, who was sitting on the floor looking very dejected.

When the Queen rushed in, and kissed her twenty times in a minute, and laughed, and cried, and told Delicia all her history, the Princess was wild with delight. Then the fairy showed her all the wonderful dresses and jewels she had brought for her, and said:

"Help, Help, I Am Pursued!"

"Don't let us waste time; we must go and address the people."

So she walked first, looking very serious and dignified, and wearing a dress the train of which was at least ten yards long. Behind her came the Queen wearing a blue velvet robe embroidered with gold, and a diamond crown that was brighter than the sun itself. Last of all walked Delicia, who was so beautiful that it was nothing short of marvelous.

They proceeded through the streets, returning the salutations of all they met, great or small, and all the people turned and followed them, wondering who these noble ladies could be.

When the audience hall was quite full, the fairy said to the subjects of the wicked King that if they would accept Delicia, who was the daughter of the jolly King, as their Queen, she would undertake to find a suitable husband for her, and would promise that during their reign there should be nothing but rejoicing and merry-making, and all dismal things should be entirely banished.

Upon this the people cried with one voice, "We will, we will, we have been gloomy and miserable too long already." And they all took hands and danced round the Queen, and Delicia, and the good fairy, singing, "Yes, yes; we will, we will!"

Then there were feasts and fireworks in every street in the town, and early the next morning the fairy, who had been all over the world in the night, brought back with her, in her flying chariot, the most handsome and good-tempered Prince she could find anywhere.

"Yes, We Will, We Will!"

His name was Prince Danilo, and his kingdom too had been wasted by the wicked king, who had made war upon it. He knew the story well of the jolly King and his family and was more than glad to join his kingdom to that of his former enemy and to rule in a spirit of both joy and harmony.

As to his getting the hand of the fair Delicia, this was as much happiness as any Prince on earth could wish for, and so he told not only the Princess herself but her tearful mother and the great good fairy who attended them both.

He was so charming that Delicia loved him from the moment their eyes met, and as for him, of course he could not help thinking himself the luckiest Prince in the world. The Queen felt that she had really come to the end of her misfortunes at last, and they all lived happily ever after.

The Luckiest Prince in the World

"Ho, Jack! Where Are You Going?"

Jack · And · The · Beanstalk

Once upon a time a boy named Jack lived with his mother on their farm. They were very poor. Although they worked very hard, the dry, rocky soil gave up barely enough to feed them and their last remaining cow, Bossy.

Although it grieved Jack's mother to do it, she decided at last that the cow must be sold. One day, she called to Jack. "There is a fair two towns away," she said, "and you Jack must go and get the best price you can for Bossy. It is impossible for us to feed her any longer, but if you go and get a good price, we should be able to live on that for at least a little while."

So off Jack went, sad to be losing so good and faithful an animal as Bossy had been, but at the same time glad enough to have a little adventure.

He hadn't gone far when suddenly a funny little man stepped out onto the road. "Ho, Jack!" the man called to him. "Where are you going with that fine looking animal?"

Jack was surprised. He wondered how this stranger knew his

name, and why he was so complimentary about Bossy, who had certainly seen better days.

"I'm off to the fair to sell my cow," Jack replied.

"Well, perhaps I can save you some steps and bother," said the little stranger. "Seeing as how I'm somewhat in the market for a cow myself."

What good luck, Jack thought. His mother would be very pleased if he managed to sell Bossy and return home so quickly. "What will you give me for her?" he asked.

"Five beans," said the stranger. "Do you know how many make five?"

"Yes," said Jack proudly. "Three in my mouth and one in each hand, that's five. But I don't know as five is enough for such a fine cow as Bossy."

"But these aren't just any five beans," the stranger said, lowering his voice and looking about as if to see if anyone else could hear him. "These are magic beans."

"Magic?" asked Jack. "What's magic about them?"

The stranger winked. "Take them home and you'll find out soon enough," he promised.

Jack wasn't quite sure. His mother wouldn't think that five beans were so much, but if they were really magic, there could be an end to all of their problems. He thought and thought, and at last made up his mind. "I'll take them!" he said to the stranger. He patted Bossy on the top of her head and handed her rope to

"These Are Magic Beans."

the stranger.

He put the beans in his pocket, turned on his heels, and headed home.

"What! So soon!" his mother said. "You must have gotten a very good price very quickly for you to be back from the fair so soon."

"I didn't even have to go all the way," said Jack proudly. "I sold Bossy, and look what I got!" He held out his hand with the five beans.

"What! You sold the whole cow for five beans!" His mother couldn't believe her ears. "That's not even enough to make supper for us!"

"But these are magic beans," Jack said. He hated when his mother was angry or disappointed with him.

"Magic! Fine! This is what I think of your magic!" And his mother grabbed the beans and threw them out of the window. She ran from the room crying, and both of them went to bed without dinner that night.

When Jack woke up in the morning, his little room was shadowed and dark. He rubbed his eyes, wondering why the bright sun that shone each morning hadn't wakened him. He went to the window and looked out. But all he could see was green, green, green, blocking out everything even up to the sky.

Jack ran outside to see what it could be.

There, towering over the house and the farm, was a

"This Is What I Think of Magic!"

beanstalk, but a beanstalk bigger than the usual kind as a king's palace was from the tiny farmhouse that Jack and his mother lived in. Stalk and leaf, branch and shoot, it reached higher into the sky than Jack could see.

"Look, Mother!" Jack said excitedly. "I told you that the beans were magic!"

"I still don't see the good of it," his mother replied. "What will it do for us to have a beanstalk that throws shadows over everything else?"

"I'm going to climb it!" Jack said. "I'm going to see what's on the very, very top!"

And climb he did. But the longer he climbed, the taller the beanstalk seemed to be. At last, quite exhausted, he reached the top.

Jack looked around. In both directions stretched a wide road. At one end, far away as it was, he could see a palace that seemed to float amidst the clouds that surrounded it.

Seeing that there was nothing in the opposite direction, Jack set off toward the palace. He walked and walked. It seemed to him as though the distance to the palace was even greater than that from the ground to the top of the beanstalk. But on and on he went, until he could make out the moat, the doors, and the windows of the tallest towers. At last he stood in front of the rough wooden bridge that stretched across the moat to the double doors of the palace entrance.

"I'm Going to Climb It!"

Everything was as still as still could be. There was no sign of life to be seen nor heard. There was nothing to do, Jack thought, but to go straight in.

He squared his shoulders, straightened his spine, and walked quickly across the bridge.

Jack could barely reach the great round rings that hung upon the doors. But grasping one as hard as he could, he pushed with all his might until the door swung open and he was inside.

Jack tiptoed cautiously along the stone corridor, peering into the enormous rooms that lined each side.

As he made his way deeper inside the palace, he heard an enormous rumbling sound coming from deep inside. Hugging the wall, he tiptoed along to see where it was coming from. As he got closer to the sound, it seemed to him as if the whole palace was shaking.

He peeked into an enormous chamber. There, on the biggest chair Jack had ever seen, sat snoring the biggest giant he could ever have imagined. The great rumbling noise was the snoring of the giant as he slept.

Jack had to hold himself very stiff to keep his knees from shaking with fright. The giant's knees were about as high as the top of Jack's head reached, and all around the red booted legs of the sleeping giant were sacks full of glittering gold coins. Some lay about on the floor, and some glittered on top of the sacks that they were crammed into. It seemed to Jack as though the giant must

He Pushed with All His Might.

have been counting his wealth and fallen asleep in the midst of the enormous inventory.

If he and his mother had only a tiny portion of the giant's wealth, it seemed to Jack they'd never have to worry about anything ever again. The thought gave him a kind of courage, and slowly, quietly, and very, very carefully he crept closer to the sleeping giant, until he was close enough to grab one of the money sacks by the ties around its neck, and shoving it inside his shirt, make his way out again as carefully as he had come in.

Jack hurried down the corridor to the palace entrance, shivering with fear as he ran every time an especially loud snore from the giant shook the palace to its very foundations.

His heart racing as fast as his legs, his legs racing as fast as his feet could carry them, at last Jack found himself on the bridge that spanned the moat and back on the road again. Even here he didn't slacken, but ran as fast as he could to where the road gave way to the top of the beanstalk.

Shifting the heavy bag of coins from side to side as he scurried down, Jack finally fell in a scramble at the bottom of the beanstalk.

He could scarcely believe he was back in his own farmyard again, so strange and bewildering had been all of the sights at the top of the beanstalk. But now he collected himself and went looking for his mother, to show her their new found treasure.

Jack's mother could scarcely believe the story of the palace

A Kind of Courage

and the giant, but when Jack emptied the bag of gold coins in front of her, she laughed and cried and declared he was the best son in the whole world. Straight away, she apologized for ever having doubted Jack and his magic beans. Now, she declared, they could live happily ever after.

"But no," said Jack. "This one bag is just the beginning of the treasures in the giant's palace. I must go back for more."

Try as she would to dissuade him, Jack was insistent. Not for one mere bag of gold had he braved the fearsome giant. There was more treasure to be had, and he was the boy to have it.

The very next morning Jack made his way back up the beanstalk. When he got to the top everything was as it had been, and he made his way quickly to the giant's palace.

Stealing inside, he passed the room where the giant was once again asleep. Ignoring the rumbling thunder of his snoring, Jack tiptoed into an enormous room that he realized was the giant's kitchen.

Enormous pots, pans, and kettles of all shapes hung about on the walls. But Jack took no interest in these. He started to walk out, to look for more treasure-laden chambers, when he spotted a plump white goose sitting on a table. Afraid that she might start honking and so awaken the giant, Jack snatched her up and tucked her under his arm.

But no sooner had he moved the goose, than she let fall a shiny egg.

Jack Snatched Her Up.

Still clutching her tightly, Jack stooped down to retrieve it. Amazingly, it hadn't broken on the hard stone floor. Jack soon realized why.

The egg was of solid gold, as bright and shiny as the coins he had gotten the previous day, but far larger.

He immediately realized the worth of this estimable bird, and headed for the beanstalk and home, knowing that this goose was the equal of any other treasure he might find.

You can imagine Jack's mother's surprise when he produced the goose and its golden outlay. Although his mother had lived on a farm all of her life, she had never seen the like.

"This bird will be our fortune, Jack!" she exclaimed. "Now we will have surely everything we need."

"Not quite yet, mother," said Jack. "For I mean to try the beanstalk yet one more time."

Nothing his mother could say would change Jack's mind, so determined was he to steal into the giant's palace once again. Thus it was that early the next morning he again made his way up the beanstalk and into the giant's castle.

Jack did not know what he might find, only he knew it would be something wondrous. Thus, when once inside the palace, he heard not the rumble of the giant's snoring, but a sweet sound drifting from above his head, he was not surprised.

Looking up, he saw a beautiful golden harp. That its shape was of a woman did not surprise him; that the harp could play

"This Bird Will Be Our Fortune!"

such wonderful music without anyone putting hands to its strings, did.

Jack had no idea what such a harp might be worth, but he knew he had to have it. He jumped up to pluck it down from the wall on which it rested. He put it under his arm and started to steal out of the palace.

But as soon as he started running, a movement like wind swept through the harp, and of its own accord it began to wail:

> "Oh master, oh master,
>
> Oh lackaday
>
> Come faster, come faster,
>
> For I'm stolen away!"

Jack ran as fast as he could, but the golden harp never ceased its wailing. The faster he ran, the louder the song became.

At last it was loud enough to rouse the sleeping giant.

The whole palace shook as Jack heard the heavy footsteps behind him.

The footsteps became faster and louder, the golden harp wailed higher and faster, and Jack's heart beat fastest of all as he raced toward the top of the beanstalk.

At last he was there. Clutching the golden harp to him, he sprang from branch to branch, making his way ever downward.

At last he reached the ground. "Mother, Mother!" he shouted. "Come quickly, and bring the old ax from the barn!"

His mother came running out. Jack took the ax from her and

"For I'm Stolen Away!"

started hacking away at the bottom of the beanstalk.

He could feel it shake and rumble, but he knew it was not from his own efforts; it was the giant, coming closer and closer. Any moment, he would be climbing down the beanstalk itself.

Jack redoubled his efforts. He chopped harder and harder.

The giant was climbing down now, his feet looking like great boulders as he placed them on lower and lower branches of the beanstalk.

Jack heaved and swung with all of his might.

The giant's bulk was blotting out the sun, and a great shadow lay over the little farm and all of the surrounding fields. The giant came closer.

With the mightiest effort he had ever made in his life, Jack swung the ax again at the very roots of the beanstalk. The weight of the giant weakened the stalk still further, and it began to sway and waver.

Suddenly, it came crashing down completely, carrying the giant with it and burying him beneath the weight of its leafy green branches.

"Oh master, oh master!" wailed the harp.

But the giant was no more.

"Oh master, oh master!" wailed the harp in a softer voice, as she turned toward Jack. "You are my master now!" she sang out.

And so saying, the harp and the goose and Jack and his mother lived in great happiness and riches forever after.

Crashing Down Completely

"Who Will Help Me Plant?"

THE · LITTLE · RED · HEN

Once upon a time a little red hen found a grain of wheat. "Who will help me plant this wheat?" she asked all the other animals in the barnyard.

"Not me," said the dog.

"Not me," said the cat.

"Not me," said the pig.

"Not me," said the turkey.

"Then I'll do it myself!" said the little red hen.

She planted the grain of wheat very carefully. In a little while, the grain took root. The wheat began to grow. Green leaves were showing on the growing stem.

Through rainy days and sunny, the little red hen watched very proudly over her wheat.

At the end of the season, the tall, strong wheat was ready to be harvested.

"Who will help me reap the wheat?" asked the little red hen.

"Not me," said the dog.

"Not me," said the cat.

"Not me," said the pig.

"Not me," said the turkey.

"I will do it myself then," said the little red hen. She got to work and soon had reaped the wheat.

But still there was more to be done.

"Who will help me thresh this wheat?" asked the little red hen.

"Not me," said the dog.

"Not me," said the cat.

"Not me," said the pig.

"Not me," said the turkey.

"Then I'll do it myself," said the little red hen. And so she did.

"Now who will help me take this wheat to the mill to grind?" asked the little red hen.

"Not me," said the dog.

"Not me," said the cat.

"Not me," said the pig.

"Not me," said the turkey.

"I'll do it myself then," said the little red hen. She carted the wheat to a nearby mill, and in a little while she came back with the grain finely ground into flour and neatly packed into a sack.

"Who will help me bake the flour?" asked the little red hen.

"Not me," said the dog.

"Who Will Help Me Grind?"

"Not me," said the cat.

"Not me," said the pig.

"Not me," said the turkey.

"Very well then, I'll do it myself," said the little red hen. Very carefully, she baked the flour into a lovely loaf of bread.

Then she asked, "Who will help me to eat this bread?"

"Me, me," said the dog.

"Me, me," said the cat.

"Me, me," said the pig.

"Me, me," said the turkey.

"Oh no, you won't!" exclaimed the little red hen.

And she ate it up all by herself!

She Ate It All Up Herself!

"The Sky's A-Falling!"

HENNY · PENNY

One day Henny Penny was picking up corn in the cornyard when — whack! — something hit her upon the head. "Goodness gracious me!" said Henny Penny; "the sky's a-going to fall; I must go and tell the King."

So she went along and she went along and she went along till she met Cocky Locky. "Where are you going, Henny Penny?" says Cocky Locky.

"Oh! I'm going to tell the King the sky's a-falling," says Henny Penny.

"May I come with you?" says Cocky Locky.

"Certainly," says Henny Penny. So Henny Penny and Cocky Locky went to tell the King the sky was falling.

They went along, and they went along, and they went along, till they met Ducky Lucky. "Where are you going to, Henny Penny and Cocky Locky?" says Ducky Lucky.

"Oh! we're going to tell the King the sky's a-falling," said Henny Penny and Cocky Locky.

"May I come with you?" says Ducky Lucky.

"Certainly," said Henny Penny and Cocky Locky. So Henny Penny, Cocky Locky, and Ducky Lucky went to tell the King the sky was a-falling.

They went along, and they went along, and they went along, till they met Goosey Loosey. "Where are you going to, Henny Penny, Cocky Locky, and Ducky Lucky?" said Goosey Loosey.

"Oh! we're going to tell the King the sky's a-falling," said Henny Penny and Cocky Locky and Ducky Lucky.

"May I come with you?" said Goosey Loosey.

"Certainly," said Henny Penny, Cocky Locky, and Ducky Lucky. Henny Penny, Cocky Locky, Ducky Lucky, and Goosey Loosey went to tell the King the sky was a-falling.

So they went along, and they went along, and they went along, till they met Turkey Lurkey. "Where are you going, Henny Penny, Cocky Locky, Ducky Lucky, and Goosey Loosey?" says Turkey Lurkey.

"Oh! we're going to tell the King the sky's a-falling," said Henny Penny, Cocky Locky, Ducky Lucky, and Goosey Loosey.

"May I come with you, Henny Penny, Cocky Locky, Ducky Lucky, and Goosey Loosey?" said Turkey Lurkey.

"Oh, certainly, Turkey Lurkey," said Henny Penny, Cocky Locky, Ducky Lucky, and Goosey Loosey. So Henny Penny, Cocky Locky, Ducky Lucky, Goosey Loosey, and Turkey Lurkey all went to tell the King the sky was a-falling.

"We're Going to Tell the King!"

They went along, and they went along, and they went along, till they met Foxy Woxy, and Foxy Woxy said to Henny Penny, Cocky Locky, Ducky Lucky, Goosey Loosey, and Turkey Lurkey, "Where are you going Henny Penny, Cocky Locky, Ducky Lucky, Goosey Loosey, and Turkey Lurkey?"

And Henny Penny, Cocky Locky, Ducky Lucky, Goosey Loosey, and Turkey Lurkey said to Foxy Woxy, "We're going to tell the King the sky's a-falling."

"Oh! but this is not the way to the King, Henny Penny, Cocky Locky, Ducky Lucky, Goosey Loosey, and Turkey Lurkey," said Foxy Woxy; "I know the proper way; shall I show it to you?"

"Oh, certainly, Foxy Woxy," said Henny Penny, Cocky Locky, Ducky Lucky, Goosey Loosey, and Turkey Lurkey.

So Henny Penny, Cocky Locky, Ducky Lucky, Goosey Loosey, Turkey Lurkey, and Foxy Woxy all went to tell the King the sky was a-falling.

So they went along, and they went along, and they went along, till they came to a narrow and dark hole. Now this was the door of Foxy Woxy's cave.

But Foxy Woxy said to Henny Penny, Cocky Locky, Ducky Lucky, Goosey Loosey, and Turkey Lurkey, "This is the short way to the King's palace; you'll soon get there if you follow me. I will go first and you come after, Henny Penny, Cocky Locky, Ducky Lucky, Goosey Loosey, and Turkey Lurkey,"

"Why, of course, certainly, without a doubt, why not?" said

"But This Is Not the Way."

Henny Penny, Cocky Locky, Ducky Lucky, Goosey Loosey, and Turkey Lurkey.

So Foxy Woxy went into his cave, and he didn't go very far, but turned round to wait for Henny Penny, Cocky Locky, Ducky Lucky, Goosey Loosey, and Turkey Lurkey. So at last, Turkey Lurkey went through the dark hole into the cave. He hadn't got far when "Hrumph," Foxy Woxy snapped off Turkey Lurkey's head and threw his body over his left shoulder.

Then Goosey Loosey went in, and "Hrumph," off went her head and Goosey Loosey was thrown beside Turkey Lurkey.

Then Ducky Lucky waddled down, and "Hrumph," snapped Foxy Woxy, and Ducky Lucky's head was off and Ducky Lucky was thrown alongside Turkey Lurkey and Goosey Loosey.

Then Cocky Locky strutted down into the cave, and he hadn't got far when "Snap! Hrumph!" went Foxy Woxy, and Cocky Locky was thrown alongside of Turkey Lurkey, Goosey Loosey, and Ducky Lucky.

But Foxy Woxy had made two bites at Cocky Locky, and when the first snap only hurt Cocky Locky, but didn't kill him, he called out to Henny Penny. But she turned tail and off she ran home, so she never told the King the sky was a-falling.

She Never Told the King.

Sultan Had Lost All His Teeth.

OLD · SULTAN

A shepherd and his wife lived and kept their flocks near a deep forest. The rest of the family consisted of their baby, and their dog Sultan. They had raised Sultan from a puppy, and he had served them good and faithfully all his life.

But now Sultan had grown quite old and had lost all his teeth. He lay resting in the grass one evening, his head on his paws. He was almost asleep, when he heard the voices of the shepherd and his wife nearby.

"We must get rid of Sultan," the shepherd was saying. "He is too old to be of any use to us. He cannot keep thieves from the house, for they would just laugh at him. He is too slow to run after the sheep, and now with all his teeth gone, he cannot even grip anything. He must go."

"But Sultan has been such a good and faithful servant all these years," the wife said. "Surely we can provide for him now that he can no longer do for us."

"No," the shepherd replied, "I've made up my mind. Tomorrow he must go. It's true that he has served us well, but that was his job after all, and he was well provided for by us all that time."

Poor Sultan could not believe his ears. It was too frightening for him to think that the very next day would be his last. Not knowing who else to turn to, he went into the forest to see his friend the wolf, who lived there.

Poor Sultan poured out his unhappy tale. The wolf listened carefully, and then thought for a while.

"I think I know what we should do," said the wolf at last. "Every day when your master and mistress go out to tend their flock, they take their child with them, and lie it down under the bushes at the edge of the forest while they are at work.

"This is what we will do," the wolf went on. "Tomorrow morning when they go to the flock, you will stay near the child, as if you are watching it. I'll come out of the forest and run away with him, and you will run after me as fast as you can. I'll put him down so that you can pick him up and carry him back. Then your master and mistress will think you saved his life, and will be so grateful to you that you can be assured of their good care for the rest of your life."

Old Sultan looked at his friend with much admiration. It would not have come into his head to devise such a scheme as this and he readily agreed to it.

The next morning, as the family went out to the flock, Old

The Wolf Listened Carefully.

Sultan trotted behind, staying with the baby as the parents went among the sheep.

He didn't have long to wait. The wolf came bounding out of the forest, and grasped the baby by his clothes in his strong jaws. As the wolf ran back into the forest, Old Sultan barked as loud as he could to make sure that his master and mistress saw what was happening.

Sure enough, the wolf put the baby down where Old Sultan could get him; when he trotted back out, carrying the baby safely, the shepherd and his wife were overjoyed and could not do enough for him.

"Old Sultan is to be given the finest dinner every day," declared the shepherd, "and what's more, he will have my own best pillow to sleep on." So saying, he bade his wife go back to their cottage to provide a wonderful meal at once.

Nor did the shepherd go back on his word. Old Sultan lived in the greatest comfort, with all that he could wish for, for a long time afterward.

One day, as Old Sultan was resting in front of the cottage, his friend the wolf reappeared.

"I helped you out when you needed me," the wolf said. "And now I need a favor in return from you, old friend."

The wolf looked around carefully, to make sure that no one else could hear them.

"Things have been difficult in the forest of late," the wolf

"The Finest Dinner Every Day!"

went on, "and I find myself in need of one of your master's good fat sheep. I will come for it in the middle of the night, but you must look the other way and tell no one."

Old Sultan shook his great shaggy head. "No," he replied, "I can not. My master and mistress have taken the best of care of me, and as long as I am with them I must be true to them."

This the wolf did not understand, and thought that Sultan was only joking. When he came back to the cottage that night, the shepherd was waiting for him. Old Sultan had been true to his word: the shepherd pounced on the wolf, hitting him hard with a short thick stick he kept for just that purpose.

The wolf was furious. "You are a traitor!" he shouted out at Sultan as he ran back toward the forest. "I will have my revenge on you yet!"

The very next day, the wolf sent a wild boar from the forest to challenge Old Sultan to a duel. The boar would be the wolf's second, and Old Sultan was to choose a second for himself as well.

Poor Sultan! There was no one else he knew to ask but an old three-legged cat that came and scratched around the shepherd's barn from time to time.

The cat agreed, although it was difficult for her; she limped along in pain, which made her hold her tail erect in the air.

The wolf and the boar were already at the agreed-upon spot, but when they saw Old Sultan and the cat approaching, they were terrified. The cat's erect tail, standing straight up in the air as it

At the Agreed-On Spot

was, they mistook for a sword that they thought Sultan was going to fight with. And when the cat limped, they thought she was picking up stones to throw at them.

This so frightened them that the boar scampered to hide behind a bush, while the wolf jumped up in a tree.

When Old Sultan and the cat arrived, they were surprised to see that no one was there.

However, the boar, being rather large in size, had not quite managed to conceal himself completely. One of his ears stuck out from behind the bush.

The cat saw it move, and thinking it was a mouse, she pounced in the air and gave it a good hard bite.

This so frightened the boar, that he jumped up and ran away, calling out as he ran, "The one in the tree, it's all his fault."

Old Sultan and the cat looked up and saw the wolf trying to hide in the branches.

Old Sultan and the cat laughed a great deal at seeing the wicked wolf in such a funny predicament.

They called him to come down, and bade him apologize.

That he did, as well as promise to lie no more, and steal no more, and so be friends again with good Old Sultan.

Friends Again

The Old Shoemaker

THE · ELVES · AND · THE · SHOEMAKER

From the Brothers Grimm

There was once a shoemaker, who, through no fault of his own, became so poor that at last he had nothing left but just enough leather to make one pair of shoes. He cut out the shoes at night, so as to set to work upon them next morning; and as he had a good conscience, he laid himself quietly down in his bed and fell asleep. In the morning, after he had said his prayers, and was going to get to work, he found the pair of shoes made and finished, and standing on his table. He was very much astonished, and could not tell what to think, and he took the shoes in his hand to examine them more clearly; they were so well made that every stitch was in its right place, just as if they had come from the hand of a master-workman.

Soon after, a purchaser entered, and as the shoes fitted him very well, he gave more than the usual price for them, so that the shoemaker had enough money to buy leather for two more pairs of shoes. He cut them out at night, and intended to set to work the next morning with fresh spirit; but that was not to be, for when he got up they were already finished, and a customer even gave him so much money that he was able to buy leather enough for four new pairs. Early next morning he found the four pairs also finished, and so it always happened; whatever he cut out in the evening was worked up by the morning, so that he was soon making a good living, and in the end became very well to do.

One night, not long before Christmas, when the shoemaker had finished cutting out, and before he went to bed, he said to his wife,

"How would it be if we were to sit up tonight and see who it is that does us this service?"

His wife agreed, and set a light to burn. Then they both hid in a corner of the room, behind some coats that were hanging up, and they began to watch. As soon as it was midnight they saw come in two neatly formed little men, who seated themselves before the shoemaker's table, and took up the work that was already prepared, and began to stitch, to pierce, and to hammer so cleverly and quickly with their little fingers that the shoemaker's eyes could scarcely follow them, so full of wonder was he. And they never left off until everything was finished and was standing ready on the table, and then they jumped up and ran off.

The next morning the shoemaker's wife said to her husband,

"Spruce and Dandy Boys Are We!"

"Those little men have made us rich, and we ought to show ourselves grateful. With all their running about, and having little to cover them, they must be very cold. I'll tell you what: I will make little shirts, coats, waistcoats, and breeches for them, and knit each of them a pair of stockings, and you shall make each of them a pair of shoes."

The husband consented willingly, and at night, when everything was finished, they laid the gifts together on the table, instead of the cut-out works, and placed themselves so that they could observe how the little men would behave. When midnight came, they rushed in, ready to set to work, but when they found, instead of the pieces of prepared leather, the neat little garments ready for them, they stood a moment in surprise, and then they showed the greatest delight.

With great swiftness they took up the pretty garments and slipped them on, singing:

"What spruce and dandy boys are we!
No longer cobblers we will be."

Then they hopped and danced about, jumping over the chairs and tables, and at last they danced out the door.

From that time they were never seen again; but it always went well with the shoemaker as long as he lived, and whatever he took in hand prospered.

Whatever he Took in Hand Prospered.

"Please Spare My Home."

THE · THREE · WISHES

O nce upon a time in a deep, dark forest there lived a poor woodsman and his wife. Every day the woodsman went out to cut down trees to make timber, and every day the work became more difficult to do.

Early one morning, after his wife had packed a meager lunch for him to take along, the woodsman started off. He went deep, deep into the forest, looking for a tree to provide him with a goodly amount of wood.

At last he spotted a great oak tree. This will make a fine day's work for me, thought the woodsman. He took his ax in both hands, swinging it over his head as he prepared to chop down the tree.

But as the ax began to descend, he heard a small voice that seemed to come from within the tree itself.

The woodsman paused in amazement, the ax stopped in mid-air. "Please, please, sir," came the voice, "do not cut down this tree, kind woodsman, please spare me my home."

The woodsman's wonder grew as from out of the very tree

itself there appeared a beautiful little spirit, standing in front of him.

The spirit repeated its plea and the woodsman, dumbfounded, at last nodded his head in agreement.

"I will do as you wish, little spirit," he said slowly, "even though it means the loss to me of a good day's work and wages."

"In doing goodness to me, I will do more than goodness to you," replied the spirit. "To show you how appreciative I am of your goodness and kindness, I will make magic for you. I will grant you the fulfillment of your next three wishes, whatsoever it may be that you wish for."

The spirit rose in the air slightly, its wings hovering, as it reached out its hand to touch the woodsman on both his shoulders. "Go now, kind man, and make your wishes with care and good thought."

The spirit disappeared, almost melting into the air, as mysteriously as it had come. The woodsman stood still for a few minutes, thoroughly dazed by all he had seen and heard. At last he recovered his senses, gathered his belongings about him, and started off through the forest for home.

As he trudged on home, his mind was full of the wonderful events of the day. He rubbed his head, wondering whether he had really seen the spirit of the tree, or if it had been a vision, or perhaps even just a dream.

All of this thinking and questioning was far more thought than he was used to, and by the time the poor woodsman found

"Make Your Wishes with Care."

himself at his own doorstep, he was thoroughly exhausted.

He went inside, wanting nothing but the comfort of his wife, his fire, and a good hot dinner.

"My, but you're home much too early for dinner to be done!" exclaimed his wife. "It lacks a good two hours before the food will be ready."

"Ah me, I wish I had a good sausage right now!" he replied.

All at once, right in front of the woodsman appeared a platter in which was sizzling as brown and perfect a sausage as he or anybody else in the world could wish for.

"How now! What is this?" asked his wife, rushing over as the fragrance of the spicy meat filled all the corners of their little house. "Where in the world did it come from?" she asked again in amazement.

It was then that the poor woodsman remembered his meeting with the spirit of the tree, and the magic that granted him his first three wishes.

"What have I done, what have I done?" the poor man groaned, holding his head in his fists. "I'd completely forgotten, and now one of my magic wishes is wasted!"

"What magic? What wishes?" his wife demanded, not understanding any of it.

It was then that he collected his senses, remembering it all, and telling her everything that had happened that afternoon.

The wife listened quietly at first, scarcely believing her ears.

"Good Sausage Right Now!"

THE THREE WISHES

But when she realized that one wish had already been wasted on the foolish sausage, her anger knew no limits.

"What have you done, what have you done?" she wailed over and over again, standing over her husband, waving her arms about as though she were going to strike him. "Look at this stupid sausage!" she exclaimed. "This is what you wished for when you might have gotten us all of the gold we could ever need for the rest of our lives, or a fine new house instead of this poor shack, or a coach and horses to drive us back and forth from the town whenever we wished?"

"I know, I know," the old man moaned, "but I was so hungry, all I could think of was something to eat. That's why I asked for the sausage."

"Sausage! Sausage indeed!" his wife shouted. "I wish the sausage was hanging from the tip of your nose right now!"

No sooner had the words left her mouth than the sausage, as if it could fly, rose up from the platter and attached itself exactly where she had wished it to be.

"Oh no, wife, oh no!" the old man cried. "Now look at what you've done!"

He started tugging at the sausage, trying to get it loose, but it was no use. Even when his wife added her hands to his, they could not move the sausage, not even a fraction of an inch.

The man looked up at his wife. "You know what it will take to remove it," he said, pleading with his voice and his eyes. "You

"From the Tip of Your Nose!"

know there will be only one way."

The wife bit her lip, and nodded. It was clear to both of them that only the third wish would be strong enough to remove the sausage from the end of the poor woodsman's nose.

The wife cocked her head, looking sharply at her husband. "You know," she said slowly, staring at him all the while, "if you look at it from a certain angle, it really doesn't look so bad at all. I warrant you would get used to it in very little time."

"Oh no, wife!" exclaimed the woodsman. "You can't be thinking that! You can't be wanting me to stay like this for the rest of my life!"

"You could get used to it," his wife said insistently. "Many folk have had to put up with much worse."

The poor man was beside himself. He knew that his wife wanted to save the third wish for one of her grand ideas. But what good would all that grandness be to him, he thought, if he were to spend the rest of his life in such a condition?

With all the strength he could summon, the poor woodsman shouted, "I wish this terrible thing was off my nose!"

Quick as a wink, there was the sausage once more, sizzling in the platter and sending forth the most delicious fragrances.

So there were no bags of gold, no horse-drawn carriages, no lofty palace for the poor woodsman and his wife. But, at least, for the day's adventure, they sat down to as fine a meal as had ever been served them!

Not That Bad from a Certain Angle

"Fill It at the Well of the World's End."

THE · WELL · OF · THE · WORLD'S · END

Once upon a time, and a very good time it was, though it wasn't in my time, nor in your time, nor any one else's time, there was a girl whose mother had died, and her father had married again. And her stepmother hated her because she was more beautiful than herself, and she was very cruel to her. She used to make her do all the servant's work, and never let her have any peace.

At last, one day, the stepmother thought to get rid of her altogether; she handed her a sieve and said to her, "Go, fill it at the Well of the World's End and bring it home to me full, or woe betide you." For she thought she would never be able to find the Well of the World's End, and, if she did, how could she bring home a sieve full of water?

Well, the girl started off, and asked every one she met to tell her where was the Well of the World's End. But nobody knew, and she didn't know what to do, when a queer little old woman, all bent double, told her where it was, and how she could get to it.

So she did what the old woman told her, and at last arrived at the Well of the World's End. But when she dipped the sieve in the cold, cold water, it all ran out again. She tried and she tried again, but every time it was the same; and at last she sat down and cried as if her heart would break.

Suddenly she heard a croaking voice, and she looked up and saw a great frog with goggle eyes looking at her and speaking to her.

"What's the matter, dearie?" it asked.

"Oh, dear, oh dear," she said, "my stepmother has sent me all this long way to fill this sieve with water from the Well of the World's End, and I can't fill it at all."

"Well," said the frog, "if you promise me to do whatever I bid you for a whole night long, I'll tell you how to fill it."

So the girl agreed, and then the frog said:

"Stop it with moss and daub it with clay,

And then it will carry the water away;"

and then it gave a hop, skip and jump, and went flop into the Well of the World's End.

So the girl looked about for some moss, and lined the bottom of the sieve with it, and over that she put some clay, and then she dipped it once again into the Well of the World's End; and this time, the water didn't run out, and she turned to go away.

Just then the frog popped up its head out of the Well of the World's End, and said, "Remember your promise."

"If You Promise, I'll Show You."

"All right," said the girl; for thought she, "what harm can a frog do me?"

So she went back to her stepmother, and brought the sieve full of water from the Well of the World's End. The stepmother was angry as can be, but she said nothing at all.

That very evening they heard something tap tapping at the door low down, and a voice cried out:

"Open the door, my honey, my heart,
Open the door, my own darling;
Mind you the words that you and I spoke,
Down in the meadow at the World's End Well."

"Whatever can that be?" cried out the stepmother, and the girl had to tell her all about it, and what she had promised the frog.

"Girls must keep their promises," said the stepmother. "Go and open the door this instant." For she was glad the girl would have to obey a nasty frog.

So the girl went and opened the door, and there was the frog from the Well of the World's End. And it hopped, and it hopped, and it jumped, till it reached the girl, and then it said:

"Lift me to your knee, my honey, my heart;
Lift me to your knee, my own darling;
Remember the words you and I spoke,
Down in the meadow by the World's End Well."

But the girl didn't like to, till her stepmother said, "Lift it up this instant! Girls must keep their promises!"

"Lift Me to Your Knee."

So at last she lifted the frog up onto her lap, and it lay there for a time, till at last it said:

"Give me some supper, my honey, my heart,

Give me some supper, my darling;

Remember the words you and I spoke,

In the meadow by the Well of the World's End."

Well, she didn't mind doing that, so she got it a bowl of milk and bread, and fed it well. And when the frog had finished, it said:

"Go with me to bed, my honey, my heart,

Go with me to bed, my own darling;

Mind you the words you spoke to me,

Down by the cold well, so weary."

But that the girl wouldn't do, till her stepmother said, "Do what you promised, girl; girls must keep their promises. Do what you're bid, or out you go, you and that froggie."

So the girl took the frog with her to bed, and kept it as far away from her as she could. Well, just as the day was beginning to break what should the frog say but:

"Chop off my head, my honey, my heart,

Chop off my head, my own darling;

Remember the promise you made to me,

Down by the cold well, so weary."

At first the girl wouldn't, for she thought of what the frog had done for her at the Well of the World's End.

But when the frog said the words over again, she went and

"Out You Go, You and Froggie."

took an ax and chopped off its head, and lo and behold, there stood before her a handsome young Prince, who told her that he had been enchanted by a wicked spell, and he could never be unspelled till some girl would do his bidding for a whole night, and chop off his head at the end of it.

The stepmother was surprised indeed when she found the young Prince instead of the nasty frog, and she wasn't best pleased, you may be sure, when the Prince told her that he was going to marry her stepdaughter because she had unspelled him.

But married they were, and went away to live in the castle of the King, his father, and all the stepmother had to console her was that it was all through her that her stepdaughter was married to a Prince.

There Was a Handsome Prince.

A Portion Under Her Sleeve

How · Sun · Moon · And · Wind · Went · Out · To · Dinner

One day Sun, Moon, and Wind went out to dine with their uncle and aunt, Thunder and Lightning. Their mother (one of the most distant Stars you see far up in the sky) waited alone for her children's return.

Now both Sun and Wind were greedy and selfish. They enjoyed the great feast that had been prepared for them without a thought of saving any of it to take home to their mother — but the gentle Moon did not forget her. Of every dish that was brought round, she placed a small portion under one of her long sleeves, that Star might also have a share in the treat.

On their return, their mother, who had kept watch for them all night long with her little bright eye, said, "Well, children, what have you brought home for me?"

Then Sun (who was eldest) said, "I have brought nothing home for you. I went out to enjoy myself with my friends — not to fetch a dinner for my mother!"

And Wind said, "Neither have I brought anything home for you, Mother. You could hardly expect me to bring a collection of good things for you, when I merely went out for my own pleasure."

But Moon said, "Mother, fetch a plate, see what I have brought you." And shaking her hands she showered down such a choice dinner as never was seen before.

Then Star turned to Sun and spoke thus, "Because you went out to amuse yourself with your friends, and feasted and enjoyed yourself, without any thought of your mother at home — you shall be cursed. Henceforth, your rays shall ever be hot and scorching, and shall burn all that they touch. And men shall hate you, and cover their heads when you appear."

(And that is why the Sun is so hot to this day.)

Then she turned to Wind and said, "You also, who forgot your mother in the midst of your selfish pleasures — hear your doom. You shall always blow in the hot, dry weather, and shall parch and shrivel all living things. And men shall avoid you from this very time."

(And that is why the Wind in the hot weather is still so disagreeable.)

But to Moon she said, "Daughter, because you remembered

Star Turned to Sun and Spoke.

your mother, and kept for her a share in your own enjoyment, from henceforth you shall be ever cool, and calm, and bright. No glare shall accompany your pure rays, and men shall always call *you* blessed."

(And that is why the Moon's light is so soft, and cool, and beautiful even to this day.)

"Cool, Calm, and Bright"

"May I Have a Bit of Bread?"

THE · GOLDEN · GOOSE

Once upon a time there was a man who had three sons. The youngest one they called the simpleton, and paid no attention to him at all unless indeed it was to laugh at him.

One day, the eldest son decided to go into the forest to cut some wood. Before he left, his mother prepared for him a loaf of bread and a flask of wine so that he might have neither hunger nor thirst.

Deep into the forest he met a little old man. "Good day to you, kind sir," said the man. "May I have a bit of the bread and wine you carry? I am very hungry and thirsty."

"If I give you of my loaf and wine, there won't be any for me," the boy answered, "so be on your way."

Leaving the little old man standing there, he went to do his work. But it wasn't long before, felling a tree with his hatchet, he would suffer dearly. The hatchet jumped up, as if of its own accord, and hit him in the arm. He had to stop working and go home for it to be tended to.

On another day, the second son went into the forest, his mother having provided food for him in much the same way as she had for his older brother. For this brother too, the little old man was waiting deep in the wood, once more begging for just a little bit of the bread and wine.

But the second son would have none of it. "Leave off, old man," he said. "If I give to you, so much the less have I for myself."

He went deeper into the forest after he had eaten and selected a tree to begin his work on.

But he was at it for only a few moments, when the hatchet jumped out of his hand and hit him in the leg, leaving him so severely wounded that there was nothing to do but limp home to be cared for.

The next day, the simpleton approached his father. "Let me go into the forest today," he said, "for my brothers have not been able to bring the wood we so sorely need."

"Off with you," scoffed his father. "If your brothers could not accomplish this, how could you, who know nothing of the work, think to do so?"

He begged and begged until his father, just to be rid of him, gave his consent. His mother prepared food and drink, not nearly so good as those she had given his brothers, and off the simpleton went.

He was surprised when he met the little old man in the

The Hatchet Jumped Out of His Hand.

woods. Concerned only with the wounds they had received and caring nothing for others, his brothers had never mentioned encountering any strangers.

But the simpleton returned the little old man's greeting kindly.

"I see you have some bread and wine," said the little old man. "I myself have neither eaten nor drunk for so many days. I wish that I may partake of your simple meal with you."

"By all means, stranger," said the simpleton. "I am more than happy to share whatever I have with you."

As they sat down to eat together in a clearing in the woods, the plain bread that the simpleton's mother had sent with him became a rich and delicious cake, and the simple everyday beverage a sparkling wine.

The young man and the old enjoyed their meal. When they had finished, the elder turned to the younger and said, "You have a good heart and a willing nature, my son. Because you have given to me, I am going to give to you. Here is a fine bit of luck for you, my young man: Look to that ancient tree yonder. When I am gone, you shall cut it down. At its roots, I promise you, you will find something very worth your while." The little old man tipped his fingers to his hat in salute, and disappeared as smoothly as he had first made himself known.

The simpleton approached the tree and chopped away at it as he had been told. Before long, it fell.

"More Than Happy to Share."

Among the tangled roots, something glittered in the sunlight. The simpleton stooped down and lifted it up in both his hands.

It was a goose, but a goose with feathers of the very purest gold. The simpleton soothed it and spoke to it and tucked it under his arm. Then he made his way to an inn where he wanted to spend the night.

He was made much of in welcome, not only by the landlord of the place, but by his three daughters as well. When they saw the golden goose, they were filled with curiosity and wonder.

The eldest daughter was seized with an urge to have, if not the goose itself, then at least one of its golden feathers. She waited and watched carefully, and when the simpleton had gone out, she grabbed the goose by one of its wings.

But when she tried to pull her hand away, she could not. She was stuck fast and could not move.

The second sister had wanted a golden feather for herself as well; but as soon as she touched her sister, she was held likewise and could not move.

When the two stricken sisters saw the youngest approach, they yelled out to her. "Stay away, stay away!" they shouted.

But she could see no reason to do so. If her sisters could make claim upon the goose, why not she?

But no sooner had she come close and barely touched with her hand the hem of her sister's sleeve, she found that she was stuck fast to her and could not turn herself loose.

Filled with Wonder and Curiosity

And that was the way they had to stay all night.

In the morning, the simpleton took leave of the inn, his goose again tucked under his arm, and he as unmindful of the three girls hanging onto it as if they didn't at all exist.

As he walked quickly along, they had to run to keep up with him.

To the right, to the left, wherever the simpleton went, the three girls had to follow him. When he zigged, they zigged; when he zagged, they zagged. Down the lanes and up the meadows, through forest and field, tired unto exhaustion, still they must follow him.

They ran along so, until they came to a field where a parson was walking. The parson, seeing the three girls in pursuit of the young man, and understanding nothing of it, was struck with dismay. "For shame, you girls, running after a young fellow in this way!" he shouted. He reached out to stop them, grasping the arm of the third sister, but he stuck fast as well and could not remove himself from the procession.

Across from the field in the churchyard, the sexton saw the parson running after the others, and he began to run, too. "Your reverence, your reverence," he called out as he tried to catch up with them. "Have you forgotten that you have a christening to do very soon?" He caught up with them and caught the parson by the hem of his coat, in order to pull him away. Alas, he found himself stuck as well, and pulled along with the others.

They Zigged, They Zagged.

As they went on, they passed two peasants hoeing in the next field. "Help, help!" shouted the sexton. "Come at once and set us free!" They dropped their hoes and ran to do his bidding, but no sooner had they touched him but they were stuck as well, and now there were seven people running along with the simpleton and the golden goose.

Soon they came to the castle of a local King. Now this King was blessed with a daughter, but the daughter herself was cursed with the burden of seriousness, a burden so heavy in her case that in all her life she had never once been known to laugh. The King was so concerned for her happiness that he had promised her hand in marriage to the first man who could cause her to laugh out loud.

Now the simpleton knew nothing of this, but when he passed by the palace with all of the seven who were following him, running, kicking, screaming, shouting, crying out for help, and performing all sorts of other antics to free themselves from their condition, the Princess burst out laughing as if she would never stop. The very peals of her laughter were like bells ringing throughout the little kingdom.

The King was very pleased at this; on the other hand, the idea of his daughter marrying a nobody like a simpleton did not seem quite right to him. Nor did he quite know what to do with the simpleton's hangers-on. After all, it was one thing for a real King to have a court and retainers of his own, but for a simpleton to be burdened with such a motley crew as this did not seem quite the royal thing.

To the Man Who Made Her Laugh

The King conferred with his ministers, and by and by they came up with a plan. In order to marry the Princess, came the royal proclamation, the simpleton must first produce a man who was able to drink up a cellar full of wine.

The simpleton set down the golden goose, enabling him to free himself of his party of people. Then he took himself back to the woods where he had first met the little old man who had led him to the goose.

At the very place where the simpleton had chopped down the tree, now sat another little old man, this one with a very sad face.

"What ails you, my friend?" the simpleton asked kindly.

"I have a thirst, but such a thirst," replied the man, "that I cannot quench. Not a keg of water, not a cask of wine, not all of heaven's droplets can quench this thirst of mine."

"Ah hah!" said the simpleton. "We are well met indeed, my friend." Then he explained to the little old man that he would give him drink by the cellar full, if only he would agree to accompany him.

This the little old man gladly did.

Straight away went they to the King's cellar. The little old man sat himself down on a small three-legged stool and the simpleton rolled vat after vat of wine in front of him.

As the whole royal court watched and wondered, the little old man drank his fill until the cellar was quite empty.

At that, the simpleton clapped his hands, and told the King

The Old Man Drank His Fill.

he was ready for his bride.

The King was more annoyed than ever. It made him wretched that such a man, called the simpleton by everybody, should be entitled to his only daughter.

Once again he conferred with the royal ministers, and once again they came up with a seemingly impossible task for the simpleton: he was now to find a man who could eat a mountain full of bread.

The simpleton put a serious face on the matter, but chuckled to himself as he hurried along back to the forest and the spot where the magic had first begun.

There sat a man who wore a barrel around his body in place of a suit of clothes. He pounded the barrel with his fists and tears ran down his face.

"Why are you so unhappy, kind sir?" asked the simpleton.

"Because, because," and the man gulped down a sob or two before he could continue, "because I am so hungry and cannot get enough to eat. Already my wife says I have eaten us out of house and home, and all the shops in my village are closed to me, because I have eaten all their wares. Yet," he went on, "I am still so hungry!"

The simpleton knew that the little old man of the forest was defending him still. "Come along with me, friend," he said, taking the poor unfortunate by the arm, "and I will take you to a kingdom where you will surely find your fill to eat."

Meanwhile, at the castle, all the granaries of the kingdom had

"Eaten Us Out of House and Home."

been emptied, all the bakeries put on triple shift to make the bread for the simpleton's next test.

When he arrived, leading the man in the barrel, all the people of the realm watched in wonder.

The simpleton bade his companion to seat himself at the base of the mountain of bread and commence to chew. As the people watched, open mouthed themselves, the mountain grew smaller and smaller, as the man fed himself happily.

The sun was beginning to set over the distant hills, and still the people stood and watched when suddenly there came a loud snapping sound.

The man had burst the staves of his barrel-suit, and the mountain of bread had completely disappeared.

The entire populace cheered and stamped their approval; people like a good show, and no one had ever entertained them quite so much as the simpleton had. They were more than happy to have him as the heir to the throne and their next King.

But the present royal majesty was having none of it. He set yet a third impossible task for the simpleton: now he must find a ship that could sail on land as well as it did on water.

Once more the simpleton went back to the place in the forest.

This time, there sat the little old man with whom he had first shared his simple meal of bread and beverage. The little man smiled at him. "I know why you are here," said he. "Because you

The Mountain of Bread Completely Disappeared.

were so kind to me when others wouldn't be, I have been pleased to help you," he said, "and now I am ready to help you again, and indeed to be with you in your moment of triumph."

With the very flick of his fingers, the little old man produced the strangest-looking contraption the simpleton had ever seen in his life. It had sticks and sails and wheels and keels and dozens of other devices going every which way; most importantly, as the little old man quickly demonstrated, it could indeed propel itself on land or water.

Soon they were making their merry way down the road toward the King's castle. When they pulled up, as you may be sure, the entire countryside emptied out to meet them.

The little old man stood at the helm, while the simpleton merely folded his arms across his chest, planted his legs firmly on the deck, and smiled out at the gaping crowd.

Soon enough, the little old man had the strange ship doing all wonder of things: it skimmed along the lake in front of the castle and then did a whirligig that brought it sailing up to the very tallest tower. Then off it went up a hill, rolling down again, splashing into the lake and stopping at last on dry land at the very feet of the King himself.

At the sight the Princess laughed more merrily than ever, the King withdrew his objections and the Princess laughed again. She gave her hand to the simpleton, and for all we know, she may be laughing still.

With the Very Flick of His Fingers

Relaxed in Front of the Fire

CAT · AND · MOUSE · TOGETHER

Once upon a time, a cat and a mouse became great friends. So much so, in fact, that the cat convinced the mouse they would do very well together were they to share everything, including a house and all its chores.

After thinking it over a little bit, the mouse agreed. After all, the cat had been more than kind to her, and inviting her to come and share his roomy house was a delight to her, she who had lived so long in just the tiniest mouse-hole.

So they agreed.

The little mouse was very good about helping her larger friend keep their new home in apple pie order. They each did what they were best at and so made equal contributions to the up-keep.

One evening, as they relaxed in front of the fire, the mouse knitting a little scarf and the cat puffing away at his pipe, the cat cleared his throat.

"I think, my dear," he said, "that it would be very well for us to give some thought to the coming of winter. It will be much more difficult for us to get food then."

"Assuredly, you are right," replied the mouse, thinking of how much more difficult it was to find her little crumbs of nourishment when the days grew cold and the nights grew long.

"It seems to me this would be a good idea," said the cat, "that we store away a little something for that time to come. I do not fancy your venturing out in winter, my dear mouse, as I would fear for your safety."

The little mouse looked up from her knitting to smile at the thoughtfulness of her kind friend.

"It seems to me," the cat went on, "that we should obtain some good food now, and put it up in a safe place so that it will be there when we need it."

The mouse readily agreed, and the two friends discussed where it would be most safe to store their supply.

After much pondering, the cat spoke up. "What could be safer than the church?" he asked. "Nobody would steal from a church."

"How right you are," said the mouse admiringly, "and how wise!"

They decided to purchase a pot of fat, whereupon the cat would place it in some hidden niche inside the great church nearby. This being done, the mouse grew even more contented with their partnership, thinking that the cat was providing her with

Purchasing a Pot of Fat

everything in the way of safety and sustenance.

The weeks went on, and the cat found himself with a great longing for the little pot of fat. If I could have just a taste of it, thought he, it would surely satisfy my curiosity as well as my appetite. So he went to the mouse. "A great thing has happened," he said, "my very dear cousin has brought a fine young kitten into the world and she wishes me most heartily to stand godfather to it. He is quite brown with the loveliest white spots, and today is the day that the christening is to be."

"How perfectly lovely!" exclaimed the mouse. "Do go along by all means, my friend. I will stay here to keep the house."

"Then I shall surely go, since you wish it," replied the cat.

"Only this, my dear," said the mouse, "pray you think of me as you are enjoying the celebration and all the good things sure to be attached to it. Perhaps you will even get some sweet red wine."

The poor little mouse! Little did she dream that there was not one whisker of truth to the cat's whole story. There was neither cousin nor kitten nor christening. But there was the church, however; for that was exactly where the cat was making his way, straight to the spot where he had hidden the little pot.

As soon as he got there, he took the top off and licked away enough of the fat to satisfy himself. Then he put it back carefully, and walked around the town, poking in and out of places, meeting up with old friends, and generally amusing himself until he thought it was time to return to the mouse and their household.

He Took the Top Off and Licked Away.

"How good to see you back!" the mouse greeted him. "Did you have a very wonderful time?"

"Well enough," replied the cat.

The little mouse was curious for all the details. "And what was the name given to the pretty kitten?" the mouse asked eagerly. "For I'm sure she was as lovely a young kitten as has ever been."

"We called her Top-off," replied the cat.

"Mercy!" exclaimed the mouse. "Top-off! What a curious name to be sure. Is it one that runs in your family?"

The cat gave as much in the way of details as necessary to satisfy the little mouse's natural curiosity, and so they went along, peacefully enough, until the cat had another great longing to be at the hidden fat.

"My dearest mouse, will wonders never cease!" the cat exclaimed one morning as the mouse busied herself sweeping out their hearthstone.

The mouse looked up from her work. "What is it, my dear friend?" she asked.

"Well a day, if another of my female connections has not gone and brought still another kitten into this world," the cat replied. "This new one, little as it is, has already got a tail that stands up like an 'S' or so I'm told. In any event, I certainly must be in attendance at the christening today, to stand godfather yet once again."

"By all means, you must," said the little mouse. "It is a very

"We Called Her Top-Off."

singular honor for you and indeed for all of your family."

At this gracious reply, the cat made a long, low bow to the mouse and swept himself out of their little home.

Straightaway he scampered to the church, pounced on the little pot of fat, and swallowed down at least half of it.

"What's done in secret tastes sweetest of all," the cat said to himself, as he licked his whiskers after the feast.

"And what name was given to the dear little one this time?" the mouse asked eagerly of the cat when he at last reached home.

"Half-gone," the cat replied.

"Half-gone!" echoed the mouse. "What a way they have with names in your family! I declare I have never heard the like!"

Before very long, the cat was so frantic to be at the fat again, he was beginning to dream about it.

"Would you believe it?" he exclaimed to the mouse one morning, "yet another one of my very close relations has been blessed with a little kitten. This one, they say, has a perfect ruff of white fur about its tiny head, although the rest of it is black as black can be."

"Imagine that," observed the mouse. "After Top-off and Half-gone, I must say I am burning with curiosity to see what name you all will put to this one!"

"As the christening is over and the celebration is done," promised the cat, "I will be here quick as light to tell you." And with that he took himself off to the church.

He Swallowed Down at Least Half.

Once again the little mouse stayed at home to clean and mend while her partner was gone.

This time the greedy cat went straightaway to the little pot and finished the fat completely.

Although he had eaten all of the fat that was meant to have seen both his partner and himself through the cold winter to come, the cat was quite pleased with himself. He felt full and satisfied and rather proud, for he knew that all that fat had given a fine, smooth sleekness to his coat. Therefore, he was in quite a good mood and easy conscience when he arrived home late that day.

"And pray tell me," said the little mouse quite excitedly, "what did you all name the latest arrival?"

"I daresay you won't be any more pleased with this one than you were with the others," said the cat. "It is called All-gone."

"All-gone!" the mouse cried out. "Such a name! Such a name! Whatever in the world can it mean?"

She shook her little head and went to sleep, not understanding any of it, but not asking any more questions about it, either.

There were no more christenings, for the winter had come hard upon them. The food supply in the little house was getting smaller every day, the mouse noticed as she cleaned and made tidy about their cupboards. But she didn't worry, knowing how the clever cat had arranged their food for the winter.

But then came the day when there was nothing more in the house. "My dear friend," she said to the cat, "the time has come

"What Did You Name the Latest?"

for us to bring in our food, which you so cleverly thought of storing for just this time. How good it is going to taste!"

"It will taste exactly the same," said the cat, staring at her, "as if you were to stick your tongue out of the window into the empty air!"

"What a strange thing to say!" cried the mouse. "I don't understand you at all!"

"Come along and you shall know it all," said the cat. So off they went to the church.

When they got there, there was the pot, but as empty as if it had never held anything.

"Now I understand!" cried the mouse. "Now I understand everything! You have deceived me wretchedly, you cat you! Now at last I know what you meant by Top-off and then Half-gone and then — "

"Not another word!" shouted the cat. "Say that other name and I will have you as well!"

The poor little mouse had "All-gone" on the very tip of her tongue, but seeing her would-be partner about to pounce, she scurried out of the way as quickly as she could. Otherwise, she knew at once, she would have been all gone, too.

She ran as fast as she could, leaving the cat and the empty pot and the church far behind.

The little mouse never looked back, and she never made a partnership with a cat ever, ever again.

She Never Looked Back.

Cloverleaf and Frivola

THE · EVIL · ENCHANTER

Once upon a time there lived a King and Queen who, though it is a very long while since they died, were much the same as people nowadays. The King, who was called Cloverleaf, liked hunting better than anything else; but he nevertheless bestowed as much care upon his kingdom as he felt equal to — that is to say, he never made an end of folding and unfolding the state documents.

As to the Queen, she had once been very pretty, and she liked to believe that she was so still, which is, of course, always made quite easy for Queens.

Her name was Frivola, and her one occupation in life was the pursuit of amusement. Balls, masquerades, and picnics followed one another in rapid succession, as fast as she could arrange them, and you may imagine that under these circumstances the kingdom was somewhat neglected.

As a matter of fact, if anyone had a fancy for a town, or a province, he helped himself to it; but as long as the King had his horses and dogs, and the Queen her musicians and her actors, they did not trouble themselves about the matter.

King Cloverleaf and Queen Frivola had but one child, and this Princess had from her very babyhood been so beautiful, that by the time she was four years old the Queen was desperately jealous of her, and so fearful that when she was grown up she would be more admired than herself, that she resolved to keep her hidden away out of sight.

To this end she caused a little house to be built not far beyond the palace gardens, on the bank of a river. This was surrounded by a high wall, and in it the charming Lucetta was imprisoned. Her nurse, who was dumb, took care of her, and the necessaries of life were conveyed to her through a little window in the wall, while guards were always pacing to and fro outside, with orders to cut off the head of anyone who tried to approach, which they would certainly have done without thinking twice about it.

The Queen told everyone, with much pretended sorrow, that the Princess was so ugly, and so troublesome, and altogether so impossible to love, that to keep her out of sight was the only thing that could be done for her. And this tale she repeated so often, that at last the whole court believed it.

Things were in this state, and the Princess was about fifteen years old, when Prince Narcissus, attracted by the report of Queen Frivola's parties, presented himself at the court. He was not much older than the Princess, and was as handsome a Prince as you

Hidden Away Out of Sight

would see in a day's journey, and really, for his age, not so very scatter-brained.

His parents were a King and Queen, who died almost at the same time, leaving their kingdom to the eldest of their children, and commending their youngest son, Prince Narcissus, to the care of the Fairy Melinette.

In this they did very well for him, for the fairy was as kind as she was powerful, and she spared no pains in teaching the little Prince everything it was good for him to know, and even imparted to him some of her own fairy lore. But as soon as he was grown up she sent him out to see the world for himself, though all the time she was secretly keeping watch over him, ready to help in any time of need.

Before he started she gave him a ring which would render him invisible when he put it on his finger.

It was in the course of the Prince's wanderings that he came to the court of Queen Frivola, where he was extremely well received. The Queen was delighted with him and so were all her ladies; and the King was very polite, though he did not quite see why the whole court was making such a fuss over him.

Prince Narcissus enjoyed all that went on, and found the time passed very pleasantly. Before long, of course, he heard the story about the Princess Lucetta, and, as it had by that time been repeated many times, and had been added to here and there, she was represented as such a monster of ugliness that he was really quite

Narcissus at Queen Frivola's Court

curious to see her, and resolved to avail himself of the magic power of his ring to accomplish his design.

So he made himself invisible, and passed the guards without their so much as suspecting that anyone was near. Climbing the wall was rather a difficulty, but when he at length found himself inside, he was charmed with the peaceful beauty of the little domain it enclosed, and still more delighted when he perceived a slender, lovely maiden wandering among the flowers.

It was not until he had sought vainly for the imaginary monster that he realized that this was the Princess herself, and by that time he was deeply in love with her, for indeed it would have been hard to find anyone prettier than Lucetta, as she sat by the brook, weaving a garland of blue forget-me-nots to crown her waving golden locks, or to imagine anything more gentle than the way she tended all the birds and beasts who inhabited her small kingdom, and who all loved and followed her.

Prince Narcissus watched her every movement, and hovered near her in a dream of delight, not daring as yet to appear to her, so humble had he suddenly become in her presence. And when evening came, and the nurse fetched the Princess into her little house, he felt obliged to go back to Frivola's palace, for fear his absence should be noticed and someone should discover his new treasure.

But he forgot that to go back absent-minded, and dreamy and indifferent, when he had before been intent and ardent about everything, was the surest way of awakening suspicion; and when,

In a Dream of Delight

in response to the jesting questions which were put to him upon the subject, he only blushed and returned evasive answers, all the ladies were certain that he had lost his heart, and did their utmost to discover who was the happy possessor of it.

As to the Prince, he was becoming day by day more attached to Lucetta, and his one thought was to attend her, always invisible, and help her in everything she did, and provide her with everything that could possibly amuse or please her.

The Princess, who had learnt to find diversion in very small things in her quiet life, was in a continual state of delight over the treasures which the Prince constantly laid where she must find them.

Then Narcissus implored his faithful friend Melinette to send the Princess such dreams of him as should make her recognize him as a friend when he actually appeared before her eyes; and this device was so successful that the Princess quite dreaded the stopping of these amusing dreams, in which a certain Prince Narcissus was such a delightful companion.

After that, he went a step further and began to have long talks with the Princess — still, however, keeping himself invisible, until she begged him so earnestly to appear to her that he could no longer resist, and after making her promise that, no matter what he was like, she would still love him, he drew the ring from his finger, and the Princess saw with delight that he was as handsome as he was agreeable.

He Drew the Ring from His Finger.

Now, indeed, they were perfectly happy, and they passed the whole long summer day in Lucetta's favorite place by the brook, and when at last Prince Narcissus had to leave her, it seemed to them both that the hours had gone by with the most amazing swiftness. The Princess stayed dreaming of her delightful Prince, and nothing could have been further from her thoughts than any trouble or misfortune, when suddenly, in a cloud of dust and shavings, came the enchanter Grumedan, and unluckily he chanced to catch sight of Lucetta.

Down he came straightway and alighted at her feet, and after one look at her charming blue eyes and smiling lips he knew that he must appear to her at once, though he was rather annoyed to remember that he had on only his second-best cloak.

The Princess sprang to her feet with a cry of terror at this sudden apparition, for really the enchanter was no beauty. To begin with, he was very big and clumsy, then he had but one eye, and his teeth were long, and he stammered badly; nevertheless, he had an excellent opinion of himself, and mistook the Princess's cry of terror for an exclamation of delighted surprise.

After pausing a moment to give her time to admire him, the enchanter made her the most complimentary speech he could invent, which, however, did not please her at all, though he was extremely delighted with it himself.

Poor Lucetta only shuddered and cried, "Oh! where is my Narcissus?"

The Enchanter Grumedan

To which he replied with a self-satisfied chuckle, "You want a narcissus, madam? Well, they are not rare; you shall have as many as you like."

Whereupon he waved his wand, and the Princess found herself surrounded and half-buried in the fragrant flowers. She would certainly have betrayed that this was not the kind of narcissus she wanted, but for the Fairy Melinette, who had been anxiously watching the interview, and now thought it quite time to interfere. Assuming the Prince's voice, she whispered in Lucetta's ear:

"We are menaced by a great danger, but my only fear is for you, my Princess. Therefore I beg you to hide what you really feel, and we will hope that some way out of the difficulty may present itself."

The Princess was much agitated by this speech, and feared lest the enchanter should have overheard it; but he had been loudly calling her attention to the flowers, and chuckling over his own smartness in getting them for her; and it was rather a blow to him when she said very coldly that they were not the sort she preferred, and she would be glad if he would send them all away.

This he did, but afterwards wished to kiss the Princess's hand as a reward for having been so obliging; but the Fairy Melinette was not going to allow anything of that kind. She appeared suddenly, in all her splendor, and cried:

"Stay, Grumedan; this Princess is under my protection, and the smallest impertinence will cost you a thousand years of captiv-

The Princess Surrounded by Flowers

ity. If you can win Lucetta's heart by the ordinary methods I cannot oppose you, but I warn you that I will not put up with any of your usual tricks."

This declaration was not at all to the enchanter's taste; but he knew that there was no help for it, and that he would have to behave well, and pay the Princess all the delicate attentions he could think of, though they were not at all the sort of thing he was used to. However, he decided that to win such a beauty it was quite worthwhile; and Melinette, feeling that she could now leave the Princess in safety, hurried off to tell Prince Narcissus what was going forward.

Of course, at the very mention of the enchanter as a rival, he was furious, and I don't know what foolish things he would not have done if Melinette had not been there to calm him down. She represented to him what a powerful enchanter Grumedan was, and how, if he were provoked, he might avenge himself upon the Princess, since he was the most unjust and churlish of all the enchanters, and had often before had to be punished by the Fairy Queen for some of his ill-deeds.

Once he had been imprisoned in a tree, and was only released when it was blown down by a furious wind; another time he was condemned to stay under a big stone at the bottom of a river, until by some chance the stone should be turned over; but nothing could ever really improve him.

The fairy finally made Narcissus promise that he would re-

Imprisoned in a Tree

main invisible when he was with the Princess, since she felt sure that this would make things easier for all of them. Then began a struggle between Grumedan and the Prince, the latter under the lead of Melinette, as to which could best delight and divert the Princess and win her love.

Prince Narcissus first made friends with all the birds in Lucetta's little domain, and taught them to sing her name and her praises, with all their sweetest trills and most touching melodies, and all day long to tell her how dearly he loved her.

Grumedan, thereupon, declared that there was nothing new about that, since the birds had sung since the world began, and all lovers had imagined that they sang for them alone. Therefore, he said, he would himself write an opera that should be absolutely a novelty and something worth hearing.

When the time came for the performance (which lasted five weary hours) the Princess found to her dismay that the "opera" consisted of this more than indifferent verse, chanted with all their might by ten thousand frogs:

"Admirable Lucetta,
   Do you think it kind or wise
   In this way to let a
   Poor enchanter hear your sighs?"

Really, if Narcissus had not been there to whisper in her ear and divert her attention, I don't know what would have become of poor Lucetta, for though the first repetition of this absurdity

Narcissus Made Friends with All the Birds.

amused her faintly, she nearly died of weariness before the time was over. Luckily Grumedan did not perceive this, as he was too much occupied in whipping up the frogs, many of whom perished miserably from fatigue, since he did not allow them to rest for a moment.

The Prince's next idea for Lucetta's amusement was to cause a fleet of boats exactly like those of Cleopatra, of which you have doubtless read in history, to come up the little river, and upon the most gorgeously decorated of these reclined the great Queen herself, who, as soon as she reached the place where Lucetta sat in rapt attention, stepped majestically on shore and presented the Princess with that celebrated pearl of which you have heard so much, saying:

"You are more beautiful than I ever was. Let my example warn you to make a better use of your beauty!"

And then the little fleet sailed on, until it was lost to view in the windings of the river. Grumedan was also looking on at the spectacle, and said very contemptuously:

"I cannot say I think these marionettes amusing. What a to-do to make over a single pearl! But if you like pearls, madam, why, *I* will soon gratify you."

So saying, he drew a whistle from his pocket, and no sooner had he blown it than the Princess saw the water of the river bubble and grow muddy, and in another instant up came hundreds of thousands of great oysters, who climbed slowly and laboriously towards her and laid at her feet all the pearls they contained.

Cleopatra Gives Lucetta the Pearl.

"Those are what I call pearls," cried Grumedan in high glee. And truly there were enough of them to pave every path in Lucetta's garden and leave some to spare! The next day Prince Narcissus had prepared for the Princess's pleasure a charming arbor of leafy branches, with couches of moss and grassy floors and garlands everywhere, with her name written in different-colored blossoms.

Here he caused a dainty little banquet to be set forth, while hidden musicians played softly, and the silvery fountains plashed down into their marble basins, and when presently the music stopped, a single nightingale broke the stillness with his delicious chant.

"Ah!" cried the Princess, recognizing the voice of one of her favorites, "Philomel, my sweet one, who taught you that new song?"

And he answered, "Love, my Princess."

Meanwhile the enchanter was very ill-pleased with the entertainment, which he declared was dullness itself.

"You don't seem to have any idea in these parts beyond little squeaking birds!" said he. "And fancy giving a banquet without so much as an ounce of silver!"

So the next day, when the Princess went out into her garden, there stood a summer-house built of solid gold, decorated within and without with her initials and the enchanter's combined. And in it was spread an enormous repast, while the table so glittered

Enough Pearls to Pave Every Path!

with golden cups and plates, flagons and dishes, candlesticks and a hundred other things beside, that it was hardly possible to look steadily at it.

The enchanter ate like six ogres, but the Princess could not touch a morsel. Presently Grumedan remarked with a grin:

"I have provided neither musicians nor singers; but as you seem fond of music I will sing to you myself."

Whereupon he began, with a voice like a screech-owl's, to chant the words of his "opera," only this time happily not at such a length, and without the frog accompaniment. After this the Prince again asked the aid of his friends the birds, and when they had assembled from all the country round, he tied about the neck of each one a tiny lamp of some brilliant color, and when darkness fell he made them go through a hundred pretty tricks before the delighted Lucetta, who clapped her little hands with delight when she saw her own name traced in points of light against the dark trees, or when the whole flock of sparks grouped themselves into bouquets of different colors, like living flowers.

Grumedan, leaning back in his arm-chair, with one knee crossed over the other and his nose in the air, looked on disdainfully.

"Oh! if you like fireworks, Princess," said he; and the next night all the will-o'-the-wisps in the country came and danced on the plain, which could be seen from the Princess's windows, and as she was looking out, and rather enjoying the sight, up sprang a

Her Name in Points of Light

frightful volcano, pouring out smoke and flames which terrified her greatly, to the intense amusement of the enchanter, who laughed like a pack of wolves quarreling.

After this, as many of the will-o'-the wisps as could get in crowded into Lucetta's garden, and by their light the tall yew-trees danced minuets until the Princess was weary and begged to be excused from looking at anything more that night.

But, in spite of Lucetta's efforts to behave politely to the tiresome old enchanter, whom she detested, he could not help seeing that he failed to please her, and then he began to suspect very strongly that she must love someone else, and that somebody besides Melinette was responsible for all the festivities he had witnessed. So after much consideration he devised a plan for finding out the truth.

He went to the Princess suddenly, and announced that he was most unwillingly forced to leave her, and had come to bid her farewell. Lucetta could scarcely hide her delight when she heard this, and his back was hardly turned before she was entreating Prince Narcissus to make himself visible once more.

The poor Prince had been getting quite thin with anxiety and annoyance, and was only too delighted to comply with her request. They greeted one another rapturously, and were just sitting down to talk over everything cozily, and enjoy the enchanter's discomfiture together, when out he burst in a fury from behind a bush.

To Bid Her Farewell

With his huge club he aimed a terrific blow at Narcissus, which must certainly have killed him but for the Fairy Melinette, who arrived on the scene just in time to snatch him up and carry him off at lightning speed to her castle in the air. Poor Lucetta, however, had not the comfort of knowing this, for at the sight of the enchanter threatening her beloved Prince she had given one shriek and fallen back insensible.

When she recovered her senses she was more than ever convinced that he was dead, since even Melinette was no longer near her, and no one was left to defend her from the odious old enchanter.

To make matters worse, he seemed to be in a very bad temper, and came blustering and raging at the poor Princess.

"I tell you what it is, madam," said he, "whether you love this whipper-snapper Prince or not doesn't matter in the least. You are going to marry me, so you may as well make up your mind to it; and I am going away this very minute to make all the arrangements. But in case you should get into mischief in my absence, I think I had better put you to sleep."

So saying, he waved his wand over her, and in spite of her utmost efforts to keep awake she sank into a deep and dreamless slumber.

As he wished to make what he considered a suitable entry into the King's palace, he stepped outside the Princess's little domain, and mounted upon an immense chariot with great solid

Just in Time!

wheels, and shafts like the trunk of an oak-tree, but all of solid gold. This was drawn with great difficulty by forty-eight strong oxen; and the enchanter reclined at his ease, leaning upon his huge club, and holding carelessly upon his knee a tawny African lion, as if it had been a little lapdog.

It was about seven o'clock in the morning when this extraordinary chariot reached the palace gates; the King was already astir, and about to set out on a hunting expedition; as for the Queen, she had only just gone off into her first sleep, and it would have been a bold person indeed who ventured to wake her.

The King was greatly annoyed at having to stay and see a visitor at such a time, and pulled off his hunting boots again with many grimaces. Meantime the enchanter was stumping about in the hall, crying:

"Where is this King? Let him be told that I must see him and his wife also."

The King, who was listening at the top of the staircase, thought this was not very polite; however, he took counsel with his favorite huntsman, and, following his advice, presently went down to see what was wanted of him. He was struck with astonishment at the sight of the chariot, and was gazing at it, when the enchanter strode up to him, exclaiming:

"Shake hands, Cloverleaf, old fellow! Don't you know me?"

"No, I can't say I do," replied the King, somewhat embarrassed.

Like a Little Lapdog

"Why, I am Grumedan, the enchanter," said he, "and I am come to make your fortune. Let us come in and talk things over a bit."

Thereupon he ordered the oxen to go about their business, and they bounded off like stags, and were out of sight in a moment. Then, with one blow of his club, he changed the massive chariot into a perfect mountain of gold pieces.

"Those are for your lackeys," said he to the King, "that they may drink my health."

Naturally a great scramble ensued, and at last the laughter and shouting awoke the Queen, who rang for her maids to ask the reason of such an unwonted hurly-burly. When they said that a visitor was asking for her, and then proceeded each one to tell breathlessly a different tale of wonder, in which she could only distinguish the words, "oxen," "gold," "club," "giant," "lion," she thought they were all out of their minds.

Meanwhile the King was asking the enchanter to what he was indebted for the honor of this visit, and on his replying that he would not say until the Queen was also present, messenger after messenger was dispatched to her to beg her immediate attendance.

But Frivola was in a very bad mood at having been so unceremoniously awakened, and declared that she had a pain in her little finger, and that nothing should induce her to come.

When the enchanter heard this he insisted that she must come.

"Those Are for Your Lackeys."

"Take my club to her Majesty," said he, "and tell her that if she smells the end of it she will find it wonderfully reviving."

So four of the King's strongest men-at-arms staggered off with it; and after some persuasion the Queen consented to try this novel remedy. She had hardly smelt it for an instant when she declared herself to be perfectly restored; but whether that was due to the scent of the wood or to the fact that as soon as she touched it out fell a perfect shower of magnificent jewels, I leave you to decide.

At any rate, she was now all eagerness to see the mysterious stranger, and hastily throwing on her royal mantle, she popped her second-best diamond crown over her night-cap, put a liberal dab of rouge upon each cheek, and holding up her largest fan before her nose — for she was not used to appearing in broad daylight — she went mincing into the great hall. The enchanter waited until the King and Queen had seated themselves upon their throne, and then, taking his place between them, he began solemnly:

"My name is Grumedan. I am an extremely well-connected enchanter; my power is immense. In spite of all this, the charms of your daughter Lucetta have so fascinated me that I cannot live without her. She fancies that she loves a certain contemptible puppy called Narcissus; but I have made very short work of him. I really do not care whether you consent to my marriage with your daughter or not, but I am bound to ask your consent, on account of a certain meddling fairy called Melinette, with whom I have

Her Second-Best Diamond Crown

reason for wishing to keep on good terms."

The King and Queen were somewhat embarrassed and did not know how to answer this terrible suitor, but at last they asked for time to talk over the matter since, they said, their subjects might think that the heir to the throne should not be married with as little consideration as a dairymaid.

"Oh, take a day or two if you like," said the enchanter, "but in the meantime, I am going to send for your daughter. Perhaps you will be able to induce her to be reasonable."

So saying, he drew out his favorite whistle, and blew one ear-piercing note — whereupon the great lion, who had been dozing in the sunny courtyard, came bounding in on his soft, heavy feet. "Orion," said the enchanter, "go and fetch me the Princess, and bring her here at once. Be gentle now!"

At these words Orion the lion went off at a great pace, and was soon at the other end of the King's gardens. Scattering the guards right and left, he cleared the wall at a bound, and seizing the sleeping Princess, he threw her onto his back, where he kept her by holding her robe in his teeth. Then he trotted gently back, and in less than five minutes stood in the great hall before the astonished King and Queen.

The enchanter held his club close to the Princess's charming little nose, whereupon she woke up and shrieked with terror at finding herself in a strange place with the detested Grumedan.

Frivola, who had stood by stiff with displeasure at the sight of

He Trotted Gently Back.

the lovely Princess, now stepped forward, and with much pretended concern proposed to carry off Lucetta to her own apartments that she might enjoy the quiet she seemed to need. Really, her one idea was to let the Princess be seen by as few people as possible; so, throwing a veil over her head, she led her away and locked her up securely.

All this time Prince Narcissus, gloomy and despairing, was kept a prisoner by Melinette in her castle in the air, and in spite of all the splendor by which he was surrounded, and all the pleasures which he might have enjoyed, his one thought was to get back to Lucetta. The fairy, however, left him there, promising to do her very best for him, and commanding all her swallows and butterflies to wait upon him and do his bidding.

One day, as he paced sadly to and fro, he thought he heard a voice he knew calling to him, and sure enough there was the faithful Philomel, Lucetta's favorite, who told him all that had passed, and how the sleeping Princess had been carried off by the lion to the great grief of all her four-footed and feathered subjects, and how, not knowing what to do, he had wandered about until he heard the swallows telling one another of the Prince who was in their airy castle and had come to see if it could be Narcissus.

The Prince was more upset than ever, and tried vainly to escape from the castle, by leaping from the roof into the clouds; but every time they caught him, and rolling softly up, brought him back to the place from which he started, so at last he gave up the

Kept a Prisoner

attempt and waited with desperate patience for the return of Melinette.

Meanwhile matters were advancing rapidly in the court of King Cloverleaf, for the Queen quite made up her mind that such a beauty as Lucetta must be got out of the way as quickly as possible. So she sent for the enchanter secretly, and after making him promise that he would never turn herself and King Cloverleaf out of their kingdom, and that he would take Lucetta far away, so that never again might she set eyes upon her, she arranged the wedding for the next day.

You may imagine how Lucetta lamented her sad fate, and entreated to be spared. All the comfort she could get out of Frivola was, that if she preferred a cup of poison to a rich husband, she would certainly provide her with one.

When, then, the fatal day came, the unhappy Lucetta was led into the great hall between the King and Queen, the latter wild with envy at the murmurs of admiration which rose on all sides at the loveliness of the Princess.

An instant later in came Grumedan by the opposite door. His hair stood on end, and he wore a huge bag-purse and a cravat tied in a bow, his mantle was made of a shower of silver coins with a lining of rose color, and his delight in his own appearance knew no bounds. That any Princess could prefer a cup of poison to himself never for an instant occurred to him.

Nevertheless, that was what did happen, for when Queen

Lucetta's Sad Fate

Frivola in jest held out the fatal cup to the Princess, she took it eagerly, crying:

"Ah! beloved Narcissus, I come to thee!" and was just raising it to her lips when the window of the great hall burst open, and the fairy Melinette floated in upon a glowing sunset cloud, followed by the Prince himself.

All the court looked on in dazzled surprise, while Lucetta, catching sight of her lover, dropped the cup and ran joyfully to meet him.

The enchanter's first thought was to defend himself when he saw Melinette appear, but she slipped round to his blind side, and catching him by the eyelashes, dragged him off to the ceiling of the hall, where she held him kicking for a while just to give him a lesson, and then touching him with her wand she imprisoned him for a thousand years in a crystal ball which hung from the roof. "Let this teach you to mind what I tell you another time," she remarked severely.

Then turning to the King and Queen, she begged them to proceed with the wedding, since she had provided a much more suitable bridegroom. She also deprived them of their kingdom, for they had really shown themselves unfit to manage it, and bestowed it upon the Prince and Princess, who, though they were unwilling to take it, had no choice but to obey the fairy. However, they took care that the King and Queen were always supplied with everything they could wish for.

Lucetta Ran Joyfully to Meet Him.

THE EVIL ENCHANTER

Prince Narcissus and Princess Lucetta lived long and happily, beloved by all their subjects. As for the enchanter, I don't believe he has been let out yet, which most folks say, and I must agree, is all to the good!

For it is the evil enchanters of this world, even the funny, clumsy ones like Grumedan, who cause most of the problems and the ills we see around us even today.

With his one eye, and that a not very good one, he failed to see that Lucetta had *no* eyes for him at all but loved only her devoted Prince Narcissus, her one true love!

Nor had the evil enchanter a pure enough heart to enable him to recognize true love when it appeared. His only thoughts were for himself, even to the point of forcing Lucetta to marry him when she didn't want to.

He even tried to make opera singers out of the poor frogs, not caring that it was against nature for frogs to sing, and other creatures to have to listen to them!

So stay, Grumedan, suspended forever in your crystal ball on the ceiling, and let your ways and your punishment be a lesson to us all!

Happy and Beloved by All

Rich in Sons

THE · HONEY · PRINCESS

Once upon a time there was a King who had three sons. The eldest two were very much alike, tall, slender and much given to foolishness. But they were paid attention to while their youngest brother, small and fair, was not given much mind.

Though rich in sons, the King was poor in land and other royal considerations. Therefore it was determined that the eldest two should set out into the world to make their fortunes.

Off they went, but not for very long. Their foolish and extravagant ways quickly led to their being completely without funds, not even the means to return home to their father and the poor kingdom.

The youngest brother begged his father to let him go out and find the missing Princes. The King resisted, having no great faith in this boy, telling him he was hardly likely to be able to make his way in the great world when it was obvious that his brothers, older and wiser, had not. But the boy begged long and loud, and at last the King relented.

The young boy set out and wherever he went stories of his brothers' foolishness reached him frequently enough that he was able to find them very quickly. He begged to be allowed to join them, to find their fortunes, and make their way back home.

At first the brothers laughed at him, that he should think himself wise enough to succeed where they had not, but at last he prevailed, and the three went off together.

They hadn't gone long when they came to a giant anthill.

"Let's pull it down," said the eldest brother, "it will be great fun to watch them jump about and try to save themselves."

"No!" insisted the youngest brother. "They are good creatures who work hard and do no one harm. We should not disturb nor injure them."

At last the older brothers left off kicking at the ant hill, and the three of them continued. They had not gone very far, however, when they came to a large pond. "Look at those fine fat ducks!" exclaimed the second brother. "Come, let us catch and roast a pair and have ourselves a fine dinner."

The eldest brother was all for it, but again the youngest protested. "Leave them alone," he demanded of his elders, "we have no right to disturb them and take their lives."

He kept on until the others heeded him and they once more made their way.

A humming, buzzing noise soon caught their attention and they stopped before a large beehive.

"Let's Pull It Down."

The fragrance of sweet honey filled the air, and so plentiful was the output of the hive that the golden liquid flowed from it on all sides.

"What fun!" laughed one of the older brothers. "Let's set it aflame and get all the honey for ourselves!"

"No, no, we mustn't," explained the youngest brother. "The bees are good folk, and do naught but pleasantness in the world. Let them do as they would, and let us go on our way."

At last he prevailed with his elders, and on they went.

Before long, the three brothers came to a castle which looked very fine. They passed by the out buildings and stables, where there were quartered many fine-looking horses; but nothing moved, for each of those noble steeds was made of marble.

There was no one to be seen, so the brothers made their way into the castle itself. From room to room they went, without seeing another soul. At last they came to a door which had three locks on the side, and a grill in the middle. Through this grill they were able to see into the next room.

There, at last, was somebody: a little dwarf sat at a table. The brothers banged on the door and shouted until at last the dwarf heard them and approached.

He said not a word, but motioned for them to follow him. He led them to a large marble table on which was set everything needed for a beautiful dinner. The dwarf motioned to the brothers to sit and partake of this repast, which they gladly did, having

"The Bees Are Good Folk."

walked from where they had seen the beehive until they came to this place, without stopping for food or drink.

When at last they had satisfied themselves at the table, the dwarf led each of them to a beautiful bedchamber, and so the three brothers past a most restful night.

The next morning, the dwarf led them to yet another room which contained yet another marble table; on this were laid three tablets which explained how the castle could be made disenchanted.

The eldest brother undertook the first task. The tablet had foretold that in the castle garden, under the soil, lay a thousand missing pearls that belonged to the King's daughter. If they could be found before sunset, the finder would both bring the castle back to life, and marry the King's daughter. But if he should fail, he himself would be turned to marble.

The eldest brother searched in the garden all day, but by the time the sun was setting had found only the first hundred of the scattered pearls, and as the sun was disappearing over the hills, its last rays shone upon him, now another marble ornament in the garden where he had been standing.

The next brother sought to complete the task on the following day, but he did no better; he found the second hundred pearls only, and became himself marble.

When it was the youngest brother's turn, he looked hard and long, but the task was so difficult, especially for one as young and

The Three Tablets

small as himself. He looked so hard and dug so deep that all his bones were aching, and at last he sat down on a large stone to rest himself.

As he sat there, along came an entire army of ants, the very ants that he had saved from his brothers' destruction.

"We have come to help you," said the King of the five thousand creatures, and before long all the pearls were heaped up in front of the youngest brother.

The dwarf was pleased enough, but then there was the next task to be fulfilled: the key to the Princess's bedchamber had been lost in the moat, and must be fished out of it again.

As the youngest brother looked down into the bottomless-appearing water, he spied two ducks, the very ones he had kept his brothers from roasting and eating. They recognized him as well, and were only too glad, upon his instructions, to turn their broad bills toward the muddy bottom and bring up the missing gold key.

When the youngest brother presented it to the dwarf, he still remained silent, only smiling and pointing with his finger to the tablet with the third, and most difficult, task of all. And this was it: The King had three daughters, all beautiful and very much alike. The eldest had eaten a tiny piece of candy, the next one a lump of sugar, and the youngest a spoonful of honey. It was the task to guess, and to win, the Princess who had eaten of the honey.

A drone and a hum was heard in the castle, and through an open window the Queen of the bees, whose hive had been saved

The Missing Gold Key

from fire by the youngest brother, flew in with all of her tribe behind her.

She, of course, could tell at once which Princess had eaten the honey. She buzzed and flew about her, so that the youngest brother could make his choice.

So the spell was broken, and all of the creatures who had been turned to marble woke from their slumbers and were alive again.

Even the two older brothers in the garden came back to their proper form.

Thus the youngest brother won his Princess, becoming the King's favorite, and succeeding him at last to the throne.

Gentle and forgiving in his nature, the youngest brother married off the elder two to his own Princess's sisters and all lived happily ever after in their new and prosperous kingdom.

She Could Tell at Once.